Mended Hearts

Mended Hearts

Alix Stokes

YellowRoseBooks
a Division of
RENAISSANCE ALLIANCE PUBLISHING, INC.
Austin, Texas

Copyright © 2000 by Alix Stokes

All rights reserved. No part of this publication may be reproduced, transmitted in any form or by any means, electronic or mechanical, including photocopy, recording, or any information storage and retrieval system, without permission in writing from the publisher.

ISBN 1-930928-01-7

First Printing 2000

9 8 7 6 5 4 3 2 1

Cover art by Lúcia A. de Nóbrega
Cover design by Mary Draganis

Published by:

Renaissance Alliance Publishing, Inc.
PMB 167, 3421 W. William Cannon Dr. # 131
Austin, Texas 78745

Find us on the World Wide Web at
http://www.rapbooks.com

Printed in the United States of America

This book is dedicated to my own soul mate, who is always there for me.

A very special thanks goes out to my best internet friend and confidant. You believed in me, in my writing, and in my story. Without your unfailing support, Mended Hearts might never have been completed.

A heartfelt thanks also goes to my beta reader, Barb Coles. You played a big role in the birth of a writer and a story. I am eternally grateful to you.

Last, but most definitely not least, I dedicate this book to my darling daughter. You patiently entertained yourself while I undertook this project. One day I expect to see you blossom as a writer in your own right.

— Alix Stokes

Prologue

August 31, 1975
Boston Children's Hospital
Surgical Floor

The tall, handsome surgeon stepped off the elevator onto the fourth floor of the hospital. A beautiful seven-year-old girl with raven hair and cerulean blue eyes followed closely behind him.

"C'mon sweetheart," he urged, taking her slender hand. She quickly obliged and gazed up at him with a smile that revealed a pair of missing front teeth. The missing teeth did nothing to detract from the child's natural beauty.

The little girl was in her element. She was making rounds with the most important person in her life—her father, who also happened to be the best pediatric heart surgeon in the country.

"Where are we going first, Dad?" she lisped as the

missing teeth affected her normally perfect enunciation.

The surgeon smiled fondly at his eldest offspring, a female copy of himself in both looks and brains. He had begun grooming her for a career in medicine at the tender age of three, and now as a precocious seven-year-old, she was more than up for the challenge.

"Let's look in on my VSD patient first."

"Okay, Dad." She looked up at him with wide, blue eyes. "That stands for Ventricular Septal Defect," the youngster announced proudly. "There's an opening in the Ventricular Septum of the heart," she continued. "Blood flows through the opening from the left ventricle to the right." Her proud father nodded, affectionately rumpling his precocious daughter's hair as she followed him into a cheery room in the pediatric unit. Disney murals decorated the lemon yellow walls.

In the middle of a large, crib-like bed sat a small, golden-haired girl. She appeared to be about four years old, with sage green eyes and long wheat colored lashes. She was dressed adorably in her best pair of pink baby doll pajamas. The child looked painfully thin, with a definite bluish tint to her lips. In her ears was a toy stethoscope, which she was using to listen to the heartbeat of her stuffed brown dog. She looked up sagely as the surgeon and his daughter approached.

"Are you gonna fix Noah's heart, too?" she asked, looking at her dog.

"Sure, little one, if you want me to." The handsome doctor leaned over the crib and put his own stethoscope on the stuffed animal, gravely nodding his head as he pretended to hear a heartbeat.

"Then can he play, and not get tired anymore?" the tot asked in a winsome, lilting voice.

"Then he'll be as good as new," the dark haired girl quipped confidently. "And so will you." She carefully climbed onto the bed with the little blonde and sat next to her. The two little girls smiled at one another and an instant bond was forged between them. One tiny hand slipped into a larger, slender one and the two small hands intertwined. "Then we can be best friends forever," the older girl declared.

"Forever." Smiling sweetly, the blonde tot leaned forward and bestowed a kiss on the older girl's cheek. "Forever and ever."

Chapter 1

24 Years Later...

> *You know that it would be untrue,*
> *You know that I would be a liar,*
> *If I were to say to you,*
> *girl we couldn't get much higher,*
> *C'mon baby light my fire,*
> *C'mon baby light my fire,*
> *Tryin' to set the night on, fire!*

The haunted strains of Jim Morrison echoed through the operating room. It was the music 31-year-old Alexandra Morgan preferred to listen to while performing surgery. Outside, a heavy thunderstorm roared, threatening the electricity. Of course, there was generator backup available at all times, but the storm still made the tall, dark haired surgeon more prickly than usual.

The ice-blue eyes narrowed as the wrong instrument was placed in her slender right hand. If looks could kill, the poor nurse assisting her would have been dead on the spot. Fortunately, she corrected her mistake quickly and Dr. Morgan decided to hold her tongue. The nurse wondered if she'd be subjected to a dressing down later. She hoped not. Almost everyone in the hospital feared the anger of the beautiful, extremely successful surgeon.

Dr. Morgan was six feet tall with long, raven hair, clear bronze skin, and crystal blue eyes. Her height alone was intimidating. Incredible beauty and keen intelligence made her even more so. But she was the best pediatric heart surgeon in the country, maybe the world, and she accepted the difficult cases no one else dared to touch. That was enough of a reason for the rest of the staff to willingly put up with her temper.

The enigmatic woman completed her residency in Massachusetts at Boston Children's Hospital, transferring to Atlanta, Georgia six months prior. Egleston Children's Hospital was naturally ecstatic to have the brilliant surgeon, a magna cum laude graduate of Harvard Medical School. Unfortunately, this excitement did not filter down to some of the staff who had to work under her. The only people she was really warm to were her patients and their families. But all rules have an exception, and the surgeon was lucky enough to have found that exception in a member of the hospital staff.

Dr. Morgan decided to close her tiny patient's incision herself today. The tall surgeon was remarkably gifted with a needle, leaving a minimal scar every time. *Little Sara might wish to wear a swimsuit someday*, she mused to herself.

Once her work was completed, Alex left the operating theater without a word to anyone. Nurse Erin Dunson breathed a huge sigh of relief that she would not be subjected to the mercurial doctor's temper that day. After washing up, Alex headed for the locker room to slip into a pair of black slacks, a black turtleneck, and black boots accentuated by a crisp, white lab coat.

Needing to check on one of her patients, two-year-old Jon Thomas, the doctor took the elevator to the Pediatric Intensive Care Unit. It was time for little Jon to be moved to a regular room. She entered the noisy, brightly lit unit and, as always, the first thing she noticed was the lilting voice of a young golden haired nurse with sage green eyes. She knew the voice well, as it belonged to twenty-eight-year old Bryn O'Neill, a Pediatric Intensive Care nurse. Although Bryn occasionally floated to the regular surgical floor, cardiac cases were her specialty. She was dedicated, warm, kind, and intelligent. More importantly, Dr. Morgan found that whenever Bryn cared for one of her small patients, they left the hospital a day earlier than usual. Since it happened with every case, she often wondered what the scientific reasoning was behind it.

Bryn knew. The young nurse was a storyteller and would have been called a bard in ancient times. It occurred to her early in her career, that telling sick children a legend or a fable might soothe their pain and fear. Her theory had proved so successful that she had written her thesis on the subject.

Dr. Morgan examined her tiny sleeping patient, and then smiled at Bryn, who continued to weave a fantastic tale throughout the child's examination. "I think this little one likes your story telling, Bryn," the tall surgeon quipped as she removed her stethoscope from her ears.

"Really? What makes you say that?" the petite nurse asked, blushing slightly.

"He's sleeping peacefully, his heart rate and blood pressure are steady, and his color's great. He's ready to be moved to a regular room."

"Ahem. I did write a thesis on the healing effects of story telling after surgery. The kids I care for do tend to go home earlier, but that's not the only reason why I tell the stories. I do it because I like to comfort them in any way I can."

Dr. Morgan smiled. "You have such a soothing voice. It seems to work minor miracles." The surgeon paused briefly, writing in her patient's chart. "I'd like to read this thesis of yours. Do you have a copy here I could look at? I just happen to have a three-day weekend coming up and some free time for a change."

"No, but I have one at home. I could run it by your house if you'd like."

"I'd like that if it's no trouble, Bryn."

"It's no trouble, Dr. Morgan," she answered softly. "If you give me a call, I'll come by after you finish your rounds."

"Thanks, I will. And please call me Alex. I've been calling you Bryn since our first lunch together, and you're still calling me Dr. Morgan."

"Okay, Alex it is then. I just...um...hate being called Nurse O'Neill. It sounds...old."

The tall, dark haired surgeon grinned crookedly.

Mended Hearts

"Bryn. I like that name." *It sounds vaguely familiar.* Alex adjusted the toddler's I.V., and then stroked little Jon's hair gently.

Bryn had been trying to figure out where she had seen Alex before. *It was odd,* she mused to herself as she watched the tender ministrations of the beautiful doctor with awe. *She doesn't seem like an Ice Princess to me.* That was the nickname some of the staff had bestowed on the woman because of her stoic, reserved attitude. Bryn didn't even want to think about the other nickname Alex had garnered—'The Breathtaking Bitch.' *Although she is breathtaking.*

"Oh, by the way. I'm listed in the phone book under E. B. O'Neill at 350 Whispering Pines Way."

"E.B. O'Neill?" Alex teased. "What does the E. stand for? That is, if you don't mind telling me."

"No, it's fine. Elizabeth."

"Well, Elizabeth Bryn O'Neill, I'll see you after work." The beautiful surgeon's smile caused Bryn's heart to skip a beat.

* * * * * * * * *

Alex Morgan was exhausted. As she changed into a worn pair of jeans and a long sleeved blue tee shirt, she felt the beginnings of a headache behind her liquid blue eyes. *Not another migraine.* She had been plagued with the God-awful headaches for years, and lately they had gotten worse.

Opening the medicine chest in her bathroom, she took a couple of pills from a bottle, filled a glass with water, and swallowed the medicine down. Looking in the mirror she noted the pallor of her face in stark contrast to her long dark tresses, visible evidence of the absolutely grueling past week. She looked forward to a long weekend off, headache or not.

She also eagerly anticipated Bryn's arrival. Bryn's sweet, outgoing, bubbly personality was what attracted Alex to her in the first place and why they had lunched together as often as possible during the past month. Alex respected the young woman for her intelligence and her devotion to her patients. Plus, she had a great deal of spunk and she didn't seem to be intimidated in the least by the stoic, dark haired woman. More importantly, she lifted the surgeon's spirits, which was something that no one else was able to do. Alex just hoped that her headache wouldn't interfere with the chance to get to know Bryn even better.

The ringing of the doorbell interrupted her thoughts. Alex hurried, as much as her headache allowed, to the front door.

"Am I early?" Bryn smiled as she glanced down at Dr. Alexandra Morgan's bare feet.

"No, you're fine. It's just...after standing on my feet all day..." She shrugged and smiled.

Bryn giggled. "I understand completely. Lots of days my feet are killing me by the end of my shift."

Bryn was dressed in a snug fitting pair of faded jeans and a sea green tank top. A green plaid shirt, worn open, topped off the look. With her long, reddish gold hair curling around her shoulders, Alex thought she looked adorable. Not for the first time, a strange sense of déjà vu washed over the doctor as she admired the young woman.

"Come on inside, Bryn. Can I get you anything?

I have coffee, soda, Snapple, wine, and Coors Lite."

"I'd like a Coke if you have one."

Hoping the caffeine would help her headache, which was getting worse, Alex took two Cokes from the refrigerator and handed one to Bryn.

As they sat down at the kitchen table, Bryn looked around, impressed by the sparkling blue and white color scheme. What little she had seen of the place appeared to be decorated in the same shades of blue and white with simple but elegant furnishings. The house was neat and organized as one might expect from the home of a surgeon.

"Thanks for coming by, Bryn." Alex smiled at the petite nurse.

"You're welcome." Bryn smiled back. "I was just planning on spending a quiet evening at home anyway. I thought maybe I'd write some more stories to tell the kids."

"By the way, did you bring the thesis?"

Bryn dug into her purse and pulled out a computer disc. "Here you go."

"Great. I can't wait to read it. I'll return it as soon as I'm finished."

"Actually, you can keep it. I made an extra copy for you."

"Thanks. I'll just go put this in my office."

By the time Alex returned and resumed her seat next to Bryn, her head was throbbing.

Sipping her Coke, Bryn noticed a chalky tinge to Alex's skin. "Alex, are you all right? You look kind of pale." She leaned over and felt Alex's forehead.

"Huh?" Alex started at the cool touch of Bryn's fingers against her skin. "I'm okay. It's just a migraine. I get them sometimes."

"Just a migraine? That seems pretty major to me. Do you need to lie down?" Bryn placed a gentle hand on Alex's shoulder.

"No, I'll be fine." Alex hated lying to Bryn but she had to keep up her stoic facade. Dr. Morgan knew of no other way to respond.

"Well, you sure don't look fine," Bryn said as she felt Alex's forehead again. "Did you take something for the pain?"

Alex put her face in her hands and rubbed her temples. "Yeah. Before you came I took something. This was just a really stressful week for me."

"I know. I heard about your heart transplant patient. Claire told me you were at the hospital until one this morning." Claire Richards, who also worked in the Pediatric Intensive Care unit, was a close friend of Bryn's. "Was it post-op bleeding?"

Alex nodded. "There was just so much scar tissue from previous surgeries. I thought I'd never get it stopped. I finally managed to though."

"I'm glad." Bryn smiled a little but her brow quickly creased in concern. She couldn't help but feel she was overstaying her visit. "You've had an exhausting week and you don't look well. I should leave so you can lie down."

"I'm okay, Bryn. Maybe I'll feel better in a little while. I'd really like for you to stay." Truthfully, Alex felt terrible. But she didn't want Bryn to leave.

"I'll stay if you want me to, but only if you lie down." *I need to stay here and make sure she's okay*, Bryn thought. *Besides, I'd love the chance to pamper her.* "Is it a deal?"

Alex decided not to waste energy arguing with the stubborn little nurse. She had heard too many rumors around the hospital about her persistence and feistiness.

"All right, Bryn." She grinned crookedly. "I'll lie down on the couch and you can keep me company." Alex was thankful she and Bryn had cultivated an easy companionship because this was one time she really didn't want to be left alone.

"Good." Before Alex could protest, Bryn had fashioned several pillows into a cozy looking bed on the couch for her. "Now lie down."

Alex raised an eyebrow at Bryn but complied anyway. Bryn plucked a soft afghan from a chair and covered the tall surgeon with it.

"There. Are you comfortable?"

Alex was amused and flattered. Here was this beautiful woman coddling her and she found herself loving the attention. "I'm very comfortable, Bryn. Thanks."

"How's the head?" Bryn kneeled beside the couch and gently touched Alex's forehead.

"It's...it's...pretty good." Alex swallowed audibly.

Bryn's sparkling green eyes peered down at her and her throat went dry. As close as they were, she could see a light dusting of very pale freckles across Bryn's cute, upturned nose. Long, wheat colored lashes brushed her cheeks whenever Bryn lowered her eyes and Alex resisted a strong urge to reach out and hug the petite blonde.

"Can I get you anything else?" Bryn asked sweetly.

"A defibrillator," Alex murmured under her breath.

"What did you say?"

"Umm...nothing, Bryn. I'd like a wet washcloth, if you don't mind. They're in the bathroom down the hall."

"Okay. I'll be back in a jiffy."

Could she be any cuter? I could be in deep waters here, Alex thought as she sighed. *Very deep waters.*

Chapter 2

Bryn quickly returned with a cool cloth and gently laid it on Alex's forehead.

"Mmm. Thanks." The surgeon closed her eyes and let out a sigh of relief. "That feels great."

"No problem. I wish I could do more. I've never had a migraine before."

"Don't start. They're definitely no fun. I've had them since I was a kid."

Wanting to stay close to her suffering friend, a sympathetically frowning Bryn sat on the floor by the couch.

"You know, I've heard some really nice things about you around the hospital. Like how you're the best heart surgeon Egleston has ever had."

Alex raised an eyebrow under the washcloth. "I'm sure that's the only nice thing you've heard," she chuckled ruefully.

"Actually, it's not. People have a lot of respect for you, Alex. They admire how good you are with your patients." Bryn paused, then giggled. "I think a few people are kind of scared of you, though."

"A few?" Alex burst out laughing, and then regretted it. She held her head in her hands and groaned. "Please don't make me laugh anymore. It hurts too much."

"I'm sorry. Will more meds help?"

Alex closed her eyes and rubbed her temples. Every beat of her heart sent stabs of pain throughout her head. If that wasn't bad enough, she was also starting to feel sick to her stomach. *Oh, God. Please don't let me throw up in front of her.*

"There's a prescription that should help, but I'm out of it."

"Well call it in and I'll go pick it up. That's one advantage of being a doctor."

Alex only hesitated a moment before making her decision. "You talked me into it. I'm starting to feel nauseated anyway. Could you hand me the phone, please?"

"Sure." Being a naturally sympathetic person, Bryn was eager to help her friend feel better, but for some reason, this felt different. Her heart ached to see Alex in such pain.

The tall surgeon called in her prescription and gave Bryn directions to the pharmacy.

"I'll be back as soon as I can," Bryn promised, suddenly not wanting to leave Alex alone.

Alex just nodded weakly, the pain and nausea making it difficult for her to talk.

Bryn broke several speed limits as she drove to

and from the pharmacy. After quickly letting herself back into the house with Alex's key, she was halfway across the living room before noticing that the couch was empty.

"Alex?" Bryn called out. "Alex?" A worried Bryn wandered through the house. Coming upon an opened door she was relieved to find a bedroom, but it was frustratingly empty. Panicking, she called out, "Alex!"

"In here," a weak voice answered. "In the bathroom."

Bryn hurried into the adjoining bathroom to find the surgeon sitting, with her back against the wall, on the floor next to the toilet. She clutched a wet washcloth in shaking hands, and her eyes were closed. Bryn felt a sharp pang in her gut at the sight of her friend's ashen face.

"Hey, are you okay?" The blonde quickly knelt next to her and took the washcloth, wet it with cool water, and gently wiped her face.

"I'm okay," she replied weakly.

"Did you vomit?"

Alex nodded, swallowing hard.

Bryn frowned, patting her shoulder gently. "I picked up your medicine. Think you can keep it down?"

"I don't know. Maybe." She shrugged.

"Okay. Let's try. I'll be right back."

The petite nurse retrieved the medication and a glass of water and brought them into the bathroom. Checking the label, she took two tiny white pills from the bottle and put them into the doctor's hand. She couldn't help but notice what incredibly beautiful hands Alex had. They appeared to be strong and soft at the same time with the long, slender fingers of a surgeon.

"Thanks," Alex whispered as Bryn held the glass to her lips. She swallowed the pills and hoped for the best.

"Let me help you to your bed now. You'll be much more comfortable there." Unable to resist the urge to comfort the woman, Bryn smoothed Alex's dark bangs away from her damp forehead. She had to admit she was a bit unnerved by seeing the strong Dr. Morgan in such a vulnerable state.

"Not yet. I might get sick again."

"Alex, maybe I should take you to the E.R. You look pretty bad."

"No, I'll be fine...if I can just keep these pills down long enough for them to work." She sighed and closed her eyes, then opened them again. "Listen, why don't you go on home, Bryn? I'm a big girl, you know."

"No. You shouldn't be alone. I'm going to stick around and take care of you until I'm absolutely certain that you're all right. Okay?" The green eyes were full of warmth and concern.

"Okay." Alex smiled wanly and closed her eyes again. Bryn slid down next to her patient. Once again she sponged Alex's face and neck, and smoothed the dark bangs away from her forehead.

Alex, who was completely unaccustomed to anyone caring for her, was surprised at how good Bryn's tender ministrations felt. After Bryn had left to pick up the prescription, Alex had run to the bathroom, making it just in time to throw up everything she had eaten that day. That, of course, had made her head throb even more. Even though she would never admit it to anyone, she hated being alone and sick. Having Bryn by her side and tending to her made her illness a little more bearable.

"How are you feeling?" Bryn asked sympathetically as she ran the cloth under cool water, wrung out the excess, and held it against the tall surgeon's forehead.

"Okay...nausea's better. I think the medicine's gonna stay down. Thanks for everything." Alex smiled weakly at Bryn.

"You're welcome. Now let's get you off this cold, hard floor and into your bed. You can barely keep your eyes open."

Alex nodded and allowed Bryn to help her stand up. The petite nurse was surprisingly strong.

When they got to the bed, Bryn pulled back the covers and helped Alex sit down. The doctor removed her jeans and got into bed wearing only her panties and tee shirt. She smiled gratefully as Bryn covered her up and fluffed her pillow.

"Feel better?"

"Mhm. This is a lot more comfortable." Alex's eyelids drooped heavily as she struggled to stay awake.

"Go to sleep now. I'll stay with you."

"Thanks. Make yourself at home." The blue eyes closed and Alex was soon fast asleep.

Bryn just stood and watched the dark beauty for a few moments. This was the first time Bryn had ever seen the very intense and focused Dr. Alexandra Morgan so relaxed and peaceful.

Maybe I'll take Alex up on her offer to make myself at home. Giving in to her tendency to eat junk food when she was at loose ends, Bryn headed for the kitchen in search of a snack.

Peeking into the surgeon's refrigerator, she found every sort of beverage imaginable. There was a choice of milk, apple juice, several flavors of Snapple, Coke, ginger ale, Coor's Lite Beer, and two bottles of Black Opal Chardonnay. Unfortunately, the only food was some hard salami and smoked Gouda cheese.

She selected a bottle of Peach Snapple and decided to check the cupboards in her hunt for food. Opening a door, her eyes grew wide at the package of chocolate Pinwheel cookies.

"Yum. My favorite." Bryn retrieved the cookies, opened the package, and placed two on a small plate she found in another cabinet.

"Well, she certainly has great taste in cookies," Bryn chuckled to herself as she savored the rich chocolate center. *Actually, she has great taste in everything.*

After finishing her snack, she wandered into Alex's office in search of something to read. A voracious reader, she learned to pick out words in the newspaper at the tender age of two. After her surgery, Bryn could read well enough to devour anything and everything to do with medicine. An I.Q. test, taken when she was a child, revealed a high intelligence. Fortunately she was a fun-loving and well-balanced individual, never taking herself too seriously.

I hope Alex doesn't mind me going into her office, Bryn said to herself. *But she did say to make myself at home.*

Dr. Morgan's office was immaculate and tastefully decorated, with polished hardwood floors covered by a large, rose-colored area rug. The walls were painted a soft gray and covered in diplomas and awards of every sort. The centerpiece of the room was a magnificent, roll top antique desk. Among several photographs adorning it was one of a very handsome man, who looked to be about thirty-five years old, holding an unmistakable young Alex in his arms. She was the spitting image of the man, who was clearly her father. They looked so happy to be in each other's company. Bryn couldn't take her eyes off the photograph. The two looked familiar somehow.

Another photo showed Alex, who appeared to be about four, with a baby boy on her lap. He looked about one year old. *Must be her brother.* He had big beautiful blue eyes like his sister but his hair was chestnut colored. The last photo was an adorable baby picture of Alex, again held by her father. The piercing blue gaze and shiny black curls were a dead giveaway to the infant's identity. Bryn chuckled as she looked at the chubby cheeks. *What an absolutely beautiful child.* Without thinking, Bryn hugged the picture to her breast. A deep emotion welled up in her heart, and tears sprang to her eyes. "What's going on with me?" she wondered aloud.

At last, she set the final photograph down. *That's odd. I wonder why there are no pictures here of her mother.* She shrugged her shoulders and turned to the shelves lining two walls to check out Alex's extensive collection of books.

Against one wall in a cherry bookcase was every

medical textbook imaginable. Most, of course, were on Pediatric Cardiology, but there were other books as well. Volumes on art, history, literature, horses, philosophy, and astronomy filled the wall of shelves.

Bryn selected *Cardiac Surgery in the Premature Infant* and wandered back into Alex's family room. Sitting in a cozy, leather recliner, she read until her own long and exhausting week caught up with her and she dozed off.

Chapter 3

Two small figures huddled in the dark. The pair of siblings always retreated to the spacious linen closet when in trouble or upset. Outside, they could hear their mother crying. That made Alex want to cry, too, but she had to be brave. David needed her.

The small boy whimpered. "I'm scared, Lexi," he whined.

"It's okay, Davy," she crooned softly. "I'll take care of you." She pulled the sobbing boy onto her lap and hugged tightly. "I'll always take care of you."

****

Bryn was awakened from a sound sleep by an earsplitting scream. Without hesitation, she bolted from the room and flew to Alex's side.

The doctor's face was flushed and beaded with sweat as she struggled to awaken from her nightmare.

"C'mon Alex, wake up. You're having a bad dream," Bryn soothed, as she gently shook the doctor. "C'mon."

Alex sat up suddenly, struggling for breath. Doing what came naturally to the young nurse, Bryn took the frightened woman in her arms and held her close.

"Oh my gosh, you're burning up," Bryn gasped in concern. She looked into Alex's glazed blue eyes. They were bloodshot and unfocused. "Damn." She gently laid the doctor's head back on her pillow. "I think we're dealing with more than just a headache here. I need to find a thermometer," she muttered before touching Alex's cheek to get her attention. "Where's your thermometer?"

"Hmm?" Alex was nearly delirious. "Medicine chest...bathroom."

Bryn hurried into the bathroom, located the thermometer, and rushed back to her patient. "Open your mouth," she ordered gently.

Alex complied meekly. The nurse sat on the edge of the bed and felt for swollen glands in her friend's neck.

"Ow." Alex winced.

"Sorry," the petite blonde murmured, more than a little disturbed by how swollen and sore the glands were.

The thermometer beeped and Bryn removed it quickly and read the results. Her sharp intake of breath confirmed Alex's suspicions. "104 degrees. Does your throat hurt?"

"A little." Alex paused, swallowing hard.

"This could be serious. I'd better get you to the

hospital."

"I don't think I'm able to get out of bed. Call my doctor. She'll make a house call."

"Okay," Bryn agreed in a shaky voice. "What's the number?"

"It's listed under Dr. Kate Taylor. Just call...information."

Bryn grabbed the phone and quickly made the call. In an effort to comfort her patient until the doctor arrived, she retrieved another cool, wet cloth and worked on bringing Alex's fever down.

"She'll be here soon. Try not to worry." Alex's lack of response did nothing to settle Bryn's rising anxiety. "Where is she?" The young nurse anxiously glanced at her watch. The ten minutes since she had placed the call felt much longer.

The doorbell finally rang and Bryn hurried to open the front door. "Come in, Dr. Taylor. I'm Bryn O'Neill, a nurse at Egleston, and a friend of Dr. Morgan's."

"Nice to meet you Bryn. I'm Dr. Katherine Taylor." She shook Bryn's hand warmly. "Please call me Kate. Now where's my patient?"

"In the bedroom. She's very ill. And it happened so fast."

Turning around after shutting the door, Bryn saw that Kate had already disappeared down the hall leading to the bedroom. *She's been here before,* the nurse mused to herself as she hurried after the doctor. Then she felt a twinge of concern at Alex's need for a doctor to make house calls.

"Alex thought she had a migraine. She took meds for it and fell asleep. Just a little while ago I heard her screaming, apparently from a nightmare. I checked her temp, and it's one-o-four," Bryn rapidly explained as Kate stood looking at a miserable Alex.

"Hey, Dr. Alex. What are you doing sick? Did one of your little kids expose you to something nasty?" Kate softly teased as she examined the groaning surgeon. "C'mon, open your mouth. I need to look in there."

"It's sore. Nothing more to see."

"Don't be such a bad patient. Now open."

"Alex, please open your mouth," Bryn pleaded.

The tall surgeon caught the earnest emerald eyes of her friend and grudgingly opened her mouth. Kate smiled at Bryn and peeked into the recalcitrant doctor's throat. "Mhm. There's your problem, Alex. You probably have strep. I need to do a throat culture to be sure."

Alex shook her head. "Go away."

Dr. Taylor opened her bag and took out a throat culture kit. "C'mon, Alex."

"Go away, Kate. If you stick that God damned thing down my throat, I swear I'll throw up on you."

Bryn couldn't help but chuckle.

Kate raised an eyebrow as she opened the kit. "I see you haven't changed one little bit. You're as cranky as ever."

"Aww, come on, Kate. You know I have strep. Just give me something for it. I'm feeling really nauseated and I mean it when I say I'll throw up on you if you poke that thing down my throat."

Kate smirked. "Okay. You win, tough stuff."

It was Bryn's turn to raise an eyebrow. She wondered if there was something between the two women.

They certainly seemed very familiar with each other. Bryn couldn't help but notice that Kate was an incredibly beautiful woman with long, auburn hair, a peaches and cream complexion, and huge brown eyes.

Dr. Taylor prepared a couple of injections to give to her patient. "Okay, Alex. Time to roll over. You haven't developed any allergies to penicillin, have you?"

Alex, as sick as she was, glared at Kate. She shook her head no, then weakly rolled over so Kate could administer the injections. "Ow. Ow. Why two shots? And you deliberately did that as hard as you could."

Kate suppressed a laugh. "I gave you something for the fever and pain since you're feeling so queasy. Don't be such a big baby." Kate packed her bag and closed it. "She's going to be just fine, Bryn. Can you stay with her until she's through the worst of it?"

"Of course. I had already planned on it," Bryn said as she wondered at the bit of jealousy she felt at the obvious rapport between the two doctors.

"Good. Call me if she gets worse. And make sure she sees me in ten days. Or I'll come looking for her."

Oh, I'll make sure. "Don't worry, I will."

"I'll let myself out. Bye, Alex. Don't give Bryn a hard time. And you might want to consider eating and sleeping once in a while. You of all people know that getting run down makes you susceptible to illness."

Alex just grunted.

After Kate left, Bryn sat down on the edge of the bed.

"Did you really mean that? About staying, that is?" Alex, struggling to keep her very heavy eyelids open, asked in a small voice.

"I'm not going anywhere." Bryn reached for Alex's hand and held it tightly. Alex closed her eyes and smiled as she fell asleep.

****

Bryn awakened slowly. Glancing over at the clock/radio with bleary eyes, she groaned at the dial reading 10:00 a.m. She had intended on waking up much earlier in case Alex needed more Tylenol, but she was just too tired, having sat up with the beautiful surgeon most of the night.

She glanced over at her peacefully sleeping friend. Stroking the smooth skin on Alex's cheek, Bryn was relieved to find it cool to the touch.

Yawning sleepily, she stood up from the comfortable chair next to her friend's bed and headed for the bathroom. After taking care of her personal needs, coffee became a priority and she padded off to the kitchen.

After putting on a pot of coffee, she busied herself with making tea for her sick patient. *I've got to get some fluids into her,* she thought as she prepared a tray for them both and walked into the bedroom. Alex was just waking up.

"Good morning," Bryn greeted cheerily. "Feeling better? I brought you some tea. Think you can keep it down? Or would you rather have some ginger ale? Or I could go to the store for some..."

Alex laughed weakly. "Good morning yourself.

Yes. Yes. No. No, the tea will be fine."

Bryn set the tray across Alex's lap. Taking a sip of tea, Alex smiled. "This is very good, Bryn. Thanks."

"You're welcome. You know, you had me really worried there for a while last night. You were one sick cookie."

"Don't remind me." Alex paused, smiling shyly. "Thanks for taking such good care of me."

"I didn't mind at all." Bryn squeezed Alex's hand. "I'm just glad you weren't alone." She released Alex's hand and sipped her coffee thoughtfully.

"I can't even remember the last time I was that sick. I'm usually pretty healthy."

Bryn sat down on the edge of the bed. "Well, what can I get for you next?" she asked cheerily. "More tea, some soup, or how about some toast? Just name it."

Alex grinned. "Shouldn't you be getting home? I mean, I'd love for you to stick around, but I already feel bad enough that you spent the whole evening looking after me. Not to mention sitting up with me all night."

"If I go home I'll just have chores to do. Besides, Dr. Taylor said I should make sure you're okay. I'm not going *anywhere* until I'm sure. So don't try and make me."

"My, aren't we the bossy one?" Alex chuckled. "But since you insist, some soup would be great."

"Consider it done." The petite blonde headed back to the kitchen, bouncing a little as she walked.

Alex sank into the soft, down pillows as she

closed her eyes. Her head still hurt a little and she was very weak. Yet, she couldn't remember when she had felt so at peace. She was certain it was due to Bryn's tender care for her when she was so sick. The young woman's willingness to drop everything and take care of her was unfathomable to the lonely surgeon.

Bryn returned with a tray bearing a bowl of chicken broth and some ginger ale. "Time for breakfast," she announced. "When you're feeling better, I'll make you something more substantial. I've been told I'm a pretty good cook."

"I'd love that," Alex returned. "I can repair holes in tiny hearts, but I'm lucky if I can boil an egg without ruining it."

Bryn laughed. "Well, I promise to make a real dinner for you as soon as you're feeling better."

"I'm gonna hold you to that promise, my friend."

Alex finished her broth. Still feeling exhausted she lay back down.

"Listen, why don't you take a nap while I go home to shower and change. I'll grab some breakfast and then come back. Okay?"

"Okay. I am tired," Alex agreed, then wryly added, "Sorry my cupboard is bare. You must be starving by now."

"I'm fine. I'll just stop by the store on my way back to pick up a few things."

Bryn tucked the tall surgeon back into the bed and fluffed up the pillows. "Need anything before I go?"

"No, I'm fine. You know, you don't need to make such a fuss just for me."

"After the night you had, you deserve a little

TLC."

Alex smiled at her nurse. "Well, I can't even remember the last time I had this much." Her pale blue eyes sparkled warmly.

Bryn assumed that Alex was exaggerating. How could a beautiful, sensitive, intelligent woman like Alexandra Morgan be lacking in tender, loving care? Sure, she had heard rumors through the hospital grapevine. Dr. Morgan was a typical surgeon: cold, stoic, controlled, and emotionless. She never allowed anyone to get close to her.

As a paradox, she was wonderfully caring to all of her patients and their families. Initially, even Bryn had found her a little on the aloof side, but that hadn't lasted very long. Bryn quickly became fond of Dr. Morgan and especially loved to watch her with the children. When it came to them, the doctor was just one big marshmallow. *Still, she has problems letting her guard down. And she hates losing control above all else.*

Bryn snapped out of her reverie. "I'll be back as soon as I can. Try and get some rest."

Noticing that Alex was asleep, Bryn tenderly stroked the doctor's bangs back, then leaned down and kissed her forehead.

Chapter 4

Upon returning, Bryn spent the remainder of the day caring for her friend and even making the promised homemade chicken soup. The two women discussed Bryn's thesis, Alex's patients, Bryn's love of baseball, cooking, and storytelling, and Alex's beloved Appaloosa gelding, Apollo. All the talk made the day pass quickly, and Alex found herself dreading the end the weekend. Not really understanding why, she was possessed with the thought that she didn't want Bryn to leave...ever.

By eleven o'clock that evening, Alex's eyelids were drooping. Bryn's soothing voice and comforting presence had all but lulled her to sleep.

"Hey, sleepyhead. I think we'd better turn in now. I'll be next door if you need anything." Alex had offered her the use of the guest bedroom when the nurse had decided to stay overnight again.

"Thanks, Bryn. For everything." She reached for

the petite blonde's hand and squeezed it. Not wanting to relinquish the contact, they held hands until Bryn reluctantly pulled hers away.

"You need to sleep now, Alex. You still have some recuperating to do. Good night." She gave her dark haired friend a quick kiss on the forehead. Alex surprised Bryn by enveloping her in a warm hug. The younger woman's heart pounded so loudly, she was afraid Alex could hear it. Returning the hug, she fought to calm her nerves.

"Night, Bryn." Alex flashed a dazzling smile at Bryn that threatened to melt her heart on the spot.

"Uh oh," the petite blonde murmured under her breath as she left the room. "Where do we go from here?"

****

The younger of two small girls was to be discharged from the hospital, having made a complete and uneventful recovery from open-heart surgery.

The two had become inseparable during the younger girl's two-week recuperation period. Rules on visitation had been relaxed or broken when the four-year-old pined for her older companion. No one wished to risk the child's health.

It wasn't hard to pull a few strings because the older girl's father was the head of Pediatric Cardiothoracic Surgery. He couldn't bear to see his usually stoic daughter cry, and did whatever he could to keep the two little girls together.

His wife didn't share his sensibilities. She was not supportive of her daughter's desire to be with her new friend, convinced that the relationship bordered on the obsessive.

The younger child's parents welcomed it, realizing that the friendship was vital to their daughter's recovery.

The two children clung tightly to one another as they prepared to say goodbye.

"Alexandra, it's time to let go," her mother chided. "Bryn and her parents have a plane to catch."

The girl ignored her mother and hugged her friend tighter, fighting back tears.

"I don't want to go, Lexi," the little blonde sobbed pathetically.

"Don't cry, Bryn," the older girl soothed. "I'll see you again. I promise."

"But I don't wanna go," the blonde tot wailed outright.

Unable to hold in her own emotions anymore, the older girl burst into tears. With both girls crying uncontrollably, all three parents stepped forward to intervene.

"That's enough of that, Alexandra. Come with me...now."

Tears spilled down the girl's beautiful little face. "I want...my...dad..." she hiccuped.

"You know he's in surgery. Now be a big girl. You're acting like a baby."

"Bye Lexi," Bryn sobbed from the comfort of her father's arms as her mother soothingly stroked her golden hair.

"Bye, Bryn," Alex mouthed as she walked out of the hospital with her mother. Her little world was *crumbling. Soon it would collapse completely.*

****

Bryn threw back the covers and leapt out of bed. Something was terribly wrong. Her heart raced, and she was overcome with an overwhelming sadness. Trying to compose herself, she couldn't shake a need to check on Alex.

"Alex, are you okay?" she whispered hesitantly as she tiptoed into the surgeon's room.

The dark haired woman, in great distress, thrashed back and forth as she struggled to awaken. Bryn sat down on the edge of the bed and shook her very gently.

Alex awakened with a start. Bryn thought she saw tears forming in those beautiful blue eyes. "Hey, what's wrong? Did you have a bad dream?" The young nurse patted her friend's shoulder sympathetically.

Clearly embarrassed, Alex quickly regained her iron composure and nodded. "I can't seem to remember it, though." She ran her fingers through the thick mane of raven hair, disgusted with her shaking hands. "I'm sorry, Bryn. Did I wake you?"

"No, I just...felt the most terrible sense of dread...and I...I just had to check on you."

Bryn's sad face tugged at Alex's heartstrings. It touched a soft spot deep within her that she didn't know she had. The tall surgeon thought for a moment, and then quickly made a decision. "Want to have a real sleepover?" Alex grinned nervously as she patted the other side of the bed, inviting Bryn to join her. Delighted with the invitation, the young woman beamed as she hopped into the huge sleigh bed.

"Feel better?" Alex asked, as she pulled the covers snugly around them.

Bryn reached for her friend's hand and held it tightly. "Much, much better." She sighed contentedly as she nestled into the soft, down bedding. "How about you?"

"I can't remember the last time I felt this good," Alex whispered as the two friends drifted off to sleep together.

****

Bryn slowly opened one eye. The first thing she was aware of was a warm weight on her chest, and the clean fragrance of Dr. Morgan's dark hair. Frowning a bit, she looked down to see Alex's right arm tucked snugly across her slim waist. The blonde smiled as she realized they had slept in one another's embrace.

Still fatigued from her illness, Alex was in a deep sleep. Bryn was reluctant to wake the sleeping doctor, but her bladder was painfully full. Carefully extricating herself from the tight embrace, she tiptoed to the bathroom.

The dark haired surgeon woke up, missing the warmth of her friend. A short time later, Bryn returned, smiling at the sleepy, disheveled appearance of the normally immaculate surgeon. The young nurse found it immensely appealing.

"Hi. How are you feeling this morning, Lex?"

One eyebrow raised in amusement. "Lex?"

"Heh. Sorry, Alex."

"Don't be." She grinned crookedly. "Someone very special used to call me that a long time ago." She looked wistful for a moment. "And I feel pretty good thanks to you and your nursing skills." Her warm smile was met with a grin from Bryn and they gazed at each other until the nurse's stomach rumbled.

"Oops." Bryn laughed. "I guess I'm hungry. What about you, Lex? You must be starved after having nothing but soup and liquids for a day."

"Actually, I am," Alex replied, as she sat up and ran a hand through her tangled, black locks.

"I'll make breakfast," Bryn offered cheerfully. "Do you feel like some coffee this morning?"

"I'd love some." Alex stretched and smiled. Bryn noticed the return of the doctor's tan coloring, and her blue eyes were clear.

Gosh, she looks good all the time, Bryn thought in amazement, *sick, with or without make-up, and when she first wakes up. Some people have all the luck.*

Alex was at that moment looking at Bryn and thinking how adorable she looked with her tousled gold hair, sparkling green eyes, and soft clear complexion. Especially in her over-sized Atlanta Braves tee shirt. Not only was she cute, she was unbelievably sweet and kind. Alex loved the way the young nurse cuddled her patients after a frightening or painful procedure. Anytime they were in need of a hug or a story she was there to provide it for them. The young nurse's big heart was the reason Alex requested for her to be assigned to all her patients' postoperative care.

While Bryn made breakfast, Alex showered and

changed into a faded pair of jeans and a long sleeved, snug fitting, white v-neck tee. Her slender feet were bare as usual.

A short while later in the kitchen, the two women sat down to coffee, fluffy scrambled eggs with cheese, bacon and toasted English muffins.

"Wow, this looks fantastic." Alex took a bite of the eggs and closed her eyes. "Mmm. It tastes even better. Thanks for making it," she said as she took another bite. "I was really hungry."

"I'm glad you like it." Bryn positively beamed. "It's really good to see you with your appetite back."

"Yeah. It feels good not to be sick."

Both women finished eating in companionable silence. As Bryn stood up to clear the table, Alex placed a hand gently on Bryn's shoulder to stop her. "You cooked, so I'll do the dishes." She gave her friend a look that broached no argument.

"No, I want you to take it easy," Bryn insisted. "You might have a relapse."

"I'm fine." The tall surgeon stood and gathered up the plates. Bryn stuck out her lower lip, not even realizing what she had done.

Alex smirked. "Is that a pout I see?" *Stick that lip back in before I kiss it,* she thought to herself.

"Huh?" Bryn asked innocently.

"Nothing," Alex chuckled. "Let's get more coffee and go out on the porch."

The two women took their mugs, and made their way to the screened in porch situated at the back of the surgeon's home. Sitting on a crisp, blue and white pinstripe loveseat, the two sipped their coffee and chatted amiably. Upon finishing her coffee, Bryn set the mug down on the deck and sighed.

"Something wrong?" Alex asked, raising an eyebrow.

"N-no, nothing's actually wrong," Bryn stammered. "It's just...I suppose I should be getting home soon." She looked down at her hands.

Alex felt a sudden pang of unexplainable melancholy. Her blue eyes clouded over with sadness for an instant before she regained her composure.

"Hey." Bryn gently touched Alex's hand in concern. "Are you okay?"

Alex thought for a moment and quickly came to a decision. "Listen, why don't you go home and get cleaned up. Then you can come back and go to the stables with me to ride Apollo. He's probably missing me by now."

"I'd love to," Bryn replied cheerfully. "I don't ride, but I could watch you."

"Great. Maybe later we can order some Chinese food for dinner and watch a movie. That is, if you'd like." Alex's big blue eyes looked hopeful.

"Sounds like a plan to me," Bryn agreed.

They took their mugs into the kitchen and put them in the dishwasher. After a brief debate with herself, Alex abandoned the idea of wasting precious time on loading the breakfast dishes into the machine. Spending that time with Bryn was much more important than such mundane matters as clean dishes. *Face it Alex,* the doctor mused to herself, *you're attracted to her.*

"I'd offer you a shower and a change of clothes, but I don't think I have anything that would fit you," Alex chuckled ruefully.

"That's okay." Bryn winked at the surgeon. "I'll be back as soon as I can."

Waiting for Bryn to return, Alex thought back over the surprising turn of events. *How could a delivery of a computer disk and a friendly visit turn into a scene with Bryn holding my head while I was sick? Last night, I even slept in her arms. Wow.* It had felt *so* good. She hadn't felt like that in a very long time.

Well, Bryn certainly didn't seem to mind, Alex thought. *In fact, she seemed to enjoy it.* She found herself wanting Bryn to hold her again.

After pulling her riding boots and helmet out of the closet, she slipped on socks and the boots, and then donned her favorite black leather jacket. Atlanta's fall weather could be warm one minute and cool the next. Alex had just finished brushing her long, ebony hair when Bryn returned.

"Ready?" Alex smiled, admiring the way Bryn's trim figure complemented the jeans, pale blue button down shirt and denim jacket she was wearing. Even the heavy black hiking boots looked good.

"I'm ready. Let's go." Bryn couldn't help but notice just how gorgeous Dr. Morgan looked in the black leather jacket. "You clean up nice," Bryn teased.

"Right back at ya." Alex tapped her on the nose gently. As the two women gazed at each other, Bryn thought she saw a flicker of recognition in her friend's eyes.

Alex cleared her throat. "The stable's just a couple of miles from here." She took the keys and lead Bryn to the gleaming, black BMW 720i SPORT parked in her garage.

The short drive to the stables was spent in companionable silence. Once there, the tall surgeon swung her long legs out of the driver's side and then opened the passenger door for Bryn. This unexpected gesture wasn't lost on the petite blonde, who smiled her thanks. She followed Alex until they came to a stall with a beautiful, dappled gray Appaloosa gelding.

The stoic doctor's face lit up as she approached her horse. "Hi, boy. Did you miss me?" He nuzzled her hair as she kissed his cheek. "I'm sorry I haven't been to see you. Wanna go for a ride?" The horse whickered in response.

Bryn stood by grinning. *If Alex's peers could see her now. She's so different away from work. Except, of course, when she's with her little patients. The Ice Princess is really a marshmallow.*

"What are you grinning at?" Alex raised an eyebrow as she continued to coo at her horse.

"Nothing. Nothing at all." Bryn tried to wipe the smile off her face, but failed.

"Not a word of this to anyone, okay?" Alex asked hopefully. "It would ruin my reputation at the hospital."

"I'll never tell, Lex." Bryn smirked as she suppressed a giggle.

"What's with this Lex thing?" Alex asked with a lopsided smile on her face.

"I don't know. It just suits you, I guess. Do you mind?"

"No, but I'll have to come up with a suitable name for you too. Like maybe, I don't know...Squeak?"

One sculpted eyebrow disappeared into the dark bangs.

Bryn gasped in mock horror. "You heard me squeak when I was stretching this morning. Didn't you?"

Alex answered with a devilish smile.

"You did. I knew it." Bryn blushed all the way to the roots of her hair. "Surely you can come up with a better nickname for me than Squeak." The blonde looked hopeful.

"We'll see," Alex replied, exceedingly pleased with herself.

After saddling Apollo, Alex led him outside the stable. With an incredible grace, she leapt up onto the strong gelding's back. Holding out a hand to Bryn, she asked, "Care to join me?"

It was tempting. Bryn wanted to, but her lack of experience with horses overruled her desires. "I think I'll pass this time," the blonde replied reluctantly.

"Okay." Alex nodded, feeling an odd sense of disappointment. "I just need to exercise him and I'll be right back."

Bryn's heart was in her throat. Something deep down inside of her stirred as she watched Alex ride off. "Uh oh," she said aloud. "I'm up a creek without the paddle." She bit her lip and swallowed audibly. *I'm falling hard.*

As Alex guided Apollo down the well-worn riding paths, she thought of Bryn. The young nurse didn't need to stay over past dinner and a movie. She was feeling fine, having recovered rather quickly from her bout with strep, probably due to Bryn's TLC. Although, she had to admit, she was still somewhat tired. At any rate, she wouldn't be in need of the young nurse's care. Alex pushed the powerful horse to a gallop. *Maybe I could have a relapse,* she thought, a wry smile creasing her face. *No, that wouldn't be fair to Bryn.* She seemed genuinely concerned when Alex was sick, and it wouldn't be right to make her worry. Besides, the young nurse was quickly becoming her closest friend and she had no intentions of jeopardizing that by being anything less than totally honest.

As Alex slowed her horse to a canter, and headed back to the stables, she wondered what Bryn had planned for her final day off. *Probably household chores,* Alex thought ruefully.

Bryn smiled sweetly as the slightly breathless Alex dismounted Apollo and led him back to the stables. The young nurse stepped forward and placed her hand on the small of Alex's back. "Hey. You're over doing things, Lex. You should be taking it easy."

"No, I'm fine. Don't worry so much, Squeak." She flashed Bryn that endearing, lopsided smile.

"Squeak?" Bryn was mildly indignant. "Cut it out, Lex."

"Here. Why don't you help me brush him down?" Alex chuckled as she handed Bryn a brush and a currycomb.

"He won't bite, will he?"

"Of course not," the surgeon emphatically answered, as she brushed the gelding. Apollo whinnied loudly, as if to answer Bryn's question, causing the petite blonde to jump, and then scoot behind Alex for protection, grabbing her around the waist.

Bryn felt Alex's laughter bubble up from deep in

her chest as she fearfully clung to the doctor. Unable to hold it back any longer, Alex burst into a fit of helpless giggles. The sound of the stoic doctor giggling made Bryn forget all about her fears. Soon, both women were laughing so hard, their sides hurt and tears rolled down their cheeks.

"Oh. My sides. That...was...too funny." Alex roared with laughter.

"You're enjoying this...way too much, Alexandra Morgan." Bryn feigned indignation.

"Oh God. The look on your...face..." Alex couldn't stop laughing.

"I hope you pee your pants," Bryn announced hopefully.

At that moment Alex stopped laughing and made a beeline for the restroom.

"Serves you right," Bryn called after her. "I hope you're too late."

A couple of minutes later Alex, still wiping her eyes and smiling, returned.

"Feel better?" Bryn teased.

"Much. I don't remember the last time I laughed like that."

"Well, I'm glad you enjoyed yourself." Bryn was really being a wonderful sport about the whole incident, and Alex found the feigned irritation extremely adorable.

"Oh God, I did. I'll never forget that face."

"Well, you had better attend to your...your horse."

"C'mon, Bryn, he won't hurt you. He's really very gentle. Come over here."

Bryn edged forward reluctantly. "He's...really, really big."

"Yeah. He's an Appaloosa gelding. Come pat him."

She gently took Bryn's hand and brought it to the Appaloosa's soft neck. The gelding whickered softly, and playfully nibbled Bryn's hair causing the small blonde to giggle.

"See, he likes you." Alex still held her hand over Bryn's small, warm fingers as she stroked the horse's neck. "You're a good boy, Apollo," the surgeon crooned.

Alex blushed when she realized her hand had not moved from Bryn's and gently pulled it back. "I think I'd better get him settled, and then we should go pick up dinner. I'm getting hungry."

"Sure. I'm pretty hungry myself," Bryn replied, feeling a little bashful.

After taking care of Apollo, Alex said goodbye, and then she and Bryn returned to the car. After they got in, Alex reached over and gave Bryn's hand a gentle squeeze. "Thanks for coming with me. I haven't had that much fun in a long time."

Bryn flushed with pleasure. "I had a great time, too, Lex. Even though you laughed at me. And I think I could actually get to like Apollo."

Alex simply smiled in response as they pulled out of the stables and drove to the Chinese restaurant.

Chapter 5

A half-hour later, they pulled into the driveway, the car filled with the fragrant aroma of Chinese food.

Back in the kitchen, Alex set out plates and silverware, while Bryn opened the fridge, peeking in. "What would you like to drink, Alex?"

"I'd like a beer, but I'd better stick to Snapple. I was dehydrated when I got sick."

"So you admit it, huh?"

"Yeah. I admit it." The surgeon smiled sheepishly.

"You need to take better care of yourself, you know."

"Now you sound like Kate," Alex teased. She sat down and picked up her chopsticks, taking a bite of sesame chicken. "Oh, this is good. Here, have a bite." She offered the tidbit to her friend. Bryn deftly snagged the chicken with her teeth.

"Mmm, you're right. That's fantastic." Bryn

joined her dark haired companion at the table, eagerly looking around for a pair of chopsticks.

"You want chopsticks?" Alex asked.

"Who can eat Chinese food without chopsticks?" Bryn chuckled.

Alex fished around in the bag and pulled out a pair, handing them to Bryn.

"Thanks, Lex. Pass the princess prawns, please?" Bryn's eyes grew wide with appreciation before diving into the succulent shrimp dish. "So tell me, Lex," Bryn began between mouthfuls of shrimp. "Why do you have such a fierce reputation at the hospital?"

Alex thought about the question before carefully answering. "I earned it," she replied matter of fact. "I'm a real bitch."

"I can't believe that," Bryn said incredulously.

"Well, believe it, because it's true," Alex replied ruefully.

"I've never seen you be nasty to anyone, Lex."

The surgeon lowered her eyes. "I hope you never do," she answered quietly.

"Well, you've always been really kind to me." Bryn took a bite of her egg roll, chewing thoughtfully.

"That's easy to do, Bryn. You're a very intelligent person, and a fantastic nurse. You give one hundred percent to your patients—all the time. Plus, you give them love. How could I not be nice to someone as special as you?" Alex sighed. "It's just...I don't suffer fools gladly."

Bryn was overwhelmed by the compliment. "Thanks, Alex. I suppose it's because I love what I do," the petite blonde said before taking another bite of sesame chicken.

"Well, it shows." Alex smiled at her, warmth sparkling in her clear blue eyes.

Bryn smiled back, and their eyes met. They could both feel something very special was happening between them, something they were powerless to stop.

"Um. I guess I'll put the food away, if you're finished." Alex, breaking away from the gaze, mumbled, clearly uncomfortable with her growing attraction to Bryn.

"Yeah, I'm done. That was great—thanks." Bryn got up to help clear the dishes and put the leftovers in the fridge.

"You ready for a movie?" Alex asked.

"Sounds good to me. What did you have in mind?"

"Well, I have a couple of old Pink Panther movies if you're interested."

"Oh, I love those movies. Inspector Clousseau cracks me up."

"Me, too," Alex replied. "Oh yeah, I almost forgot. Want dessert?"

"I always want dessert, Lex." Bryn's beautiful green eyes sparkled.

"Do you like Pinwheels?"

"Love them." Bryn looked sheepish for a moment. "Um...actually I...I've already been into your stash of Pinwheels."

Alex grinned. "When?"

"When you were so sick the other night."

Alex burst out laughing. "Don't worry about it, silly. I always share my cookies with my friends." The surgeon looked directly into Bryn's eyes.

Bryn smiled and squeezed her hand. "I consider

you a friend, too, Lex—a very good one. And I can't believe we both love the same brand of cookie."

"Me either. After all, Pinwheels aren't your garden variety cookies."

Alex put four cookies on a plate and took it into the family room while Bryn carried their beverages. As they sat on the couch, their legs touched and neither made a move away from each other.

Dessert was consumed as they watched the movie. Noticing a chocolate smudge on her companion's full lips, Alex took a napkin and playfully wiped it off. It took all the willpower she could muster not to kiss the chocolate smudge away. Bryn was awakening all sorts of feelings within her, emotions she hadn't felt in years.

Bryn realized she was holding her breath. Alex's beautiful blue eyes were locked on her, and they were so close, she could feel the doctor's warm breath on her face. She inhaled deeply, and Alex gently pulled back, breaking the spell—for the moment.

Returning their attention to the movie, they each reveled in the companionable closeness, amazed at how comfortable it felt. The movie was over all too quickly, and both were thinking of a way to prolong their evening together as the credits rolled rapidly by.

"Would you like some coffee?" Alex asked hopefully. "I do coffee really well."

"I'm always up for coffee, Lex."

After they returned to the kitchen, Alex ground fresh coffee beans and poured filtered water into her coffeemaker as Bryn watched from the table. While the coffee was brewing, the doctor retrieved a container of half-and-half from the fridge and put it in front of a grinning Bryn. Pouring the fragrant beverage into two huge latte mugs and setting one before Bryn, Alex couldn't help but grin as the blonde added lots of cream and sugar. Alex preferred her coffee the same way.

"So, do you have family here?" Alex asked, sipping her coffee thoughtfully.

"Yes, I do. My mom, dad, and a younger sister, Cameron."

"Are you close?" Alex was genuinely interested.

"Oh yeah. Very close," Bryn replied proudly. "What about you?"

Alex paused, looking for the right words. "They're all in Boston. But, no. Actually I'm...I'm estranged from them."

"Oh, Lex, I'm so sorry." *Damn, I stuck my foot in it,* Bryn thought.

"It's all right. It's probably better this way. My mother and I never could get along anyway."

"You want to talk about it?" Bryn laid a small, warm hand on the tall surgeon's forearm.

"Maybe some other time," Alex promised.

"What made you come to Atlanta? After all, Boston has some great hospitals."

Alex shrugged. "I just really needed a change." *Like getting away from a lot of bad memories. Who are you kidding, Alex?* "Plus, it was a great professional opportunity. And with the nice weather, I can ride my horse year round."

"Yeah. I love it here. Of course, I've been here my whole life."

"Say, would you like to go to a Braves game with me this Saturday? I have a couple of tickets, and they're dug-out seats."

"You don't have to ask me twice." Bryn flushed with pleasure.

"I'm a Red Sox fan myself, but now that I'm in Atlanta, I suppose it couldn't hurt to root for the home team."

Bryn laughed. "I'll make a Braves fan out of you yet."

"We'll see." Alex smirked.

"Well, I think I should be going. If you're sure you're feeling okay."

"I'm great, as good as new. I really appreciate you looking after me. It couldn't have been a whole lot of fun."

"Well, it wasn't fun seeing my best friend so sick. I was really worried about you. But honestly, I liked taking care of you. It made me feel...better."

Alex's mouth fell open. Then her faced glowed with the sweetest, most beautiful smile Bryn had ever seen. "Best friend, huh?"

"Yep. Best friend." Bryn reached over and intertwined her fingers with Alex's.

"Um...Bryn, I really hate to see you go." Alex's heart was in her throat. "I've never felt so comfortable around anyone before." Her blue eyes were filled with warmth as they captured Bryn's startled but pleased eyes.

"Same here. It's really strange, but I feel anxious about leaving."

"Then don't. We both have tomorrow off. I mean, if you want to stay, that is," Alex added, betraying an endearing vulnerability.

"I'd like that, Lex." Bryn smiled, crinkling her

nose ever so slightly.

"You know, Bryn, you're so cute when you do that." The tall surgeon gently tapped the tip of the petite blonde's nose with her finger.

Bryn blushed from her neck all the way to the roots of her blond hair. "I...I am?" she stammered and swallowed nervously.

"Yes, you are," Alex assured her.

"Well...um...thanks, Lex. You're pretty cute yourself."

Alex laughed heartily. "Well, I don't think anyone's ever called me cute before, but I'll take that as a compliment."

The fall evening was so beautiful, they decided to take their coffee and more cookies out to the loveseat on the screened in porch. Much to their surprise they sat up talking and holding hands all night. As the two became even better acquainted, Alex was able to coax much more out of Bryn about her life than Bryn was able to with Alex. The surgeon was hesitant to discuss certain things, and Bryn, being a sensitive soul, did not want to push.

Around five in the morning, Alex fell asleep, her head in Bryn's lap. Absently stroking the long silky hair, Bryn couldn't remember how Alex's head ended up in her lap, but she didn't care. She only knew that she loved the way it felt. Soon, she was lulled to sleep by the tall surgeon's deep, even breathing.

****

Gray light filtered onto the porch. Dark lashes fluttered and blue eyes opened. It took Alex a moment to figure out where she was.

Her limbs were stiff and uncomfortable, but she felt very much at peace. She looked up into the sweet, sleeping face of Bryn, her cheeks flushed with sleep, and smiled. Carefully standing, she stretched the stiffness from her long arms and legs.

"Bryn, wake up. C'mon." Alex shook her gently. "Let's go lie down on my bed. You don't look very comfortable."

"Huh? Ahhhhh," Bryn squeaked as she stretched.

Alex grinned. "There you go making cute noises again. C'mon, let's go."

Bryn got up and obediently followed Alex into her bedroom. After taking off her boots and socks, she joined the ever bare-footed Alex in the big sleigh bed. Bryn sleepily pulled Alex close, cuddling her like a huge teddy bear. Instantly, she fell fast asleep.

Alex chuckled. "What am I? A stuffed animal? Oh well, if I can be your stuffed animal, then that's fine by me." Soon she was sleeping peacefully as well.

It would prove to be the last happy moment of the day.

****

It was close to 9:00 a.m. when Alex's pager vibrated noisily on her bedside table. With Bryn still clinging to her, she groaned and reached for it. She retrieved the number and picked up the bedside phone, dialing quickly.

Bryn awakened to the deep, resonant tones of Alex's voice and struggled to open her eyes.

"This is Dr. Morgan." Alex paused, listening. "You mean the VSD repair?" The surgeon's beautiful face looked grim. "I'll be there as soon as I can."

Alex jumped out of bed and went into the bathroom. After washing her face and brushing her teeth, she ran a brush through her thick, black mane, and then tied it back in a loose ponytail.

Bryn walked in sleepily as Alex applied blush and a soft shade of lipstick. "What's up?" she asked, yawning.

"My Ventricular Septal Defect patient. He's having complications," she replied grimly.

The color quickly drained from Bryn's face. "Uh oh. What kind of complications?"

"He's running a temp, and he's developed a cough."

"You mean Will? That cute little two year old?"

"Yeah, it's Will," Alex replied ruefully.

"I'll make some coffee while you change clothes. I don't want you getting a migraine on top of everything else that's happening."

"Thanks, Bryn." Alex smiled gratefully.

In five minutes, Alex came into the kitchen wearing black dress slacks and a powder blue silk blouse. To Bryn's eyes she looked stunning, despite the fact that she was running on only four hours of sleep.

Bryn rummaged around in the cupboard and found a commuter cup, which she filled with fresh coffee; prepared just the way Alex preferred. "I hope Will is going to be okay, Lex," she said softly with a worried look on her face as she handed the doctor the cup.

"Me too, Bryn," Alex sighed, taking the coffee and giving Bryn a little hug. "Thanks for this.

You're a really thoughtful person."

"You're welcome. It's really no big deal," Bryn said modestly.

"Well, I appreciate it. I guess I'd better get going. I'll see you at the hospital tomorrow?"

Bryn nodded. "And Lex?"

"Hmm?"

"Please call and let me know how Will is doing."

"Sure thing. Well, thanks again for everything."

"I was happy to do it. Don't worry about me, I'll let myself out."

Alex gave Bryn another quick hug, which was willingly returned, before leaving what was left of her weekend behind.

Chapter 6

By the time Alex arrived at the hospital, her young patient had developed a fulminating pneumonia, despite the state of the art care. Alex sat at his bedside and tried to comfort his distraught parents. She believed that this kind of personal involvement was vital to her patient's recovery. It provided the hospital staff their only opportunity to witness a thawing out of the Ice Princess.

"I thought he was getting better," Anne Blake sobbed as she stroked her young son's hair. "You said this was a fairly routine surgery. But...look at him. He's dying, isn't he? Tell us the truth, Dr. Morgan." The young mother tearfully collapsed in her husband's arms.

"Anne, Mike, let's step outside. William may be able to hear you, even though he's unconscious. And please, call me Alex?" she asked softly, as she laid a gentle hand on the young mother's shoulder.

The sad trio stepped into the surgeon's private office. Alex offered coffee to the parents as she steeled herself for what was the hardest part of her job. Ignoring the gnawing pain in her gut, she took a deep breath and said, "I don't think I have to tell you how ill your son is. He's lapsed into a coma, and the next step is to place him on a respirator."

Anne and Mike Blake clung to one another, crying in fear and shock.

"The decision to place your son on life support will ultimately be up to you. The chances of recovery at this point are slim to none. In my professional opinion, the respirator will only prolong his pain and suffering." Alex bowed her head, her dark brows furrowing in pain. "Sometimes it's just better to let go," she finished softly, her voice cracking slightly.

"No," the young mother screamed. "I won't. You have to do everything in your power to save him. He's only two years old. Don't you understand?" Anne hysterically pleaded as she fell on her knees in front of Alex. Her husband stepped forward to intervene.

Blue eyes flashed with emotion. "I'll do everything in my power to save Will, but the odds are stacked heavily against him. But it's your decision. I can arrange to have him placed on a respirator immediately." Alex's head started pounding, and she discreetly reached into her drawer for her medicine. Swallowing a couple of pills and rubbing the back of her neck, she couldn't shake her feeling of helplessness. *Goddamn. I hate to see my patients suffer. But, if he were your child, Alex, wouldn't you try everything possible to save him? Even if you knew it was hopeless?*

"Thank you, Dr. Morgan," Anne Blake sniffled as she regained her composure. "Mike, we need to be with our son now. Let's go." They put on a brave face and walked arm in arm out of Alex's office.

Why the fuck are you thanking me? Your son doesn't stand a snowball's chance in hell. Once Alex was certain that the Blakes were gone, she closed the door. Walking calmly back to her desk, she proceeded to pick up a glass water pitcher, and slam it into the wall. After numbly staring at the splotches of water and scattered shards of glass for several minutes, the frustrated surgeon picked up the phone. "This is Alexandra Morgan. I need a respiratory therapist to P.I.C.U. immediately." She sighed deeply, trying to catch her breath. "Oh yes, one more thing. Can you send a janitor to my office right away?"

Sometimes all the kindness, dedication, brilliance and education in the world can't sway what the fates have already decreed. William Blake died around 11:00 p.m. that day, taking with him a piece of Dr. Morgan's confidence in her ability to save lives.

After informing the grief stricken parents, a devastated Alex numbly changed back into street clothes and drove home. *You fucked up royally this time, Alexandra. What will Bryn think?* The idea of having to tell the softhearted nurse was almost as painful to her as the news itself.

Upon arriving home, she immediately picked up the phone. Glancing at the clock, she realized it was after 1:00 a.m. and she hesitated. But Bryn had asked to be informed of the child's well being, and Alex *always* kept her word.

The slim blonde answered on the first ring, having sat up reading and drinking hot chocolate while she waited for news.

The tall surgeon's voice was hoarse and strained, and Bryn scarcely recognized it. "Lex? Is that you?" A cold fear gripped Bryn's gut.

"Bryn...there's no easy way to say this. Will...died around eleven o'clock." Alex sighed deeply.

"What? Oh no." Bryn burst into tears. "How?"

"Fulminating pneumonia," Alex answered flatly.

"Oh God. His poor parents," Bryn responded before focusing on Alex's lifeless tone. It sounded like the surgeon was in shock. Pulling her emotions together, she announced, "Alex, I'm coming over right now."

"No, Bryn, I'm all right. He isn't the first patient I've lost, and I'm sure he won't be the last—considering the cases I take." Alex's voice was completely emotionless, and it frightened Bryn.

The petite nurse had a definite stubborn streak. "I'll be there in about fifteen minutes."

"Suit yourself," she replied, hanging up the phone. Alex tried to sound noncommittal, but she was secretly grateful, needing Bryn's company more than ever.

The surgeon trudged into the bathroom, undressing and stepping into the shower. Her throat was tight from holding in her emotions. While trying to wash her day away, she thought back to a conversation she once had with Kate. *You know, Alex, one day you are going to simply explode from holding your feelings in. That, or have a nervous breakdown. I only hope someone's around to pick up the pieces.* Alex had sternly asked Kate not to *ever* analyze her again. And the good Dr. Taylor never brought up the subject again.

When there was no more hot water, Alex stepped out of the shower stall, quickly dried off, and slipped into a pair of blue French terry sweat shorts with a matching top. As usual, her slender feet were bare. She absently combed the tangles out of her long hair, letting it dry naturally.

The doorbell rang just as Alex was opening a bottle of Coors Lite. Hurriedly opening the door, Alex was not prepared to see Bryn's tear stained face and it tugged at her heartstrings.

"I'm so sorry, Lex." Bryn enveloped Alex in a warm hug.

Alex couldn't believe how good it felt to have Bryn hold her. She wanted to break down and cry, but she never allowed herself that luxury, fearing she might never be able to stop. The pain inside her was just too great.

The two women held each other for a long time, each drawing comfort from the other. Finally, Alex suggested they go to the screened in porch for some fresh air. "Want a beer or something, Bryn?"

"I'll just have a cup of tea, please."

After Alex prepared the tea for Bryn, they took their beverages to the porch. The atmosphere of the porch had always soothed Alex, and she often spent time there after grueling days, which were more numerous than the surgeon would have liked.

Alex sat down on the pinstripe loveseat and rested her long legs on the coffee table.

"You look exhausted, Lex," Bryn commented as she joined the surgeon. Reaching out, she tucked a lock of dark hair behind Alex's ear.

"I am pretty tired. Today was...a real bitch."

"I'm so sorry." She stroked Alex's hair. "What went wrong?"

"Will developed a really bad pneumonia. It happens sometimes." Alex took a sip of her beer.

"It's not your fault, Lex." The nurse gently rubbed Alex's arm.

"I know, but I still feel responsible." *I bet that never happened to Dad. I guess you're not so perfect after all, Dr. Morgan. Olivia warned you that you would never be as good as your father. Apparently, she was right.*

"Lex? Are you okay? You kind of zoned out on me there."

"Huh?" Alex snapped out of her reverie. "I'm okay. I just keep wondering what I did wrong. After all, this was a routine surgery."

"Listen. You're a wonderful doctor. Don't ever think that you're not. I know that you did everything you could."

Alex looked down, and for a moment Bryn thought the doctor might cry. She actually hoped Alex would, knowing how devastated her friend was. Bryn knew the benefit of healing tears, and she sensed that Alex carried a lot of pain inside her. Putting her arm around the broad shoulders she softly said, "If you need to cry, I'm here for you." She rubbed Alex's back soothingly. "And I won't tell anyone."

Alex smiled ruefully. "Thanks, Bryn. But I'm not even sure I know how anymore." She drained the last of her beer and sighed.

"Maybe you should learn."

"Maybe."

Bryn sensed it was time to change the subject. "Alex, when was the last time you ate?"

Alex looked confused. "I can't remember. Last night, I think."

"Let me fix you something. You'll feel better if you eat."

"I don't think I can, Bryn. My stomach has been tied up in knots today. But thanks."

"Lex, you're exhausted. And you've just gotten over a nasty bout of strep. Now I'm going to fix you some soup and put you to bed. Soup should go down easy."

Alex smiled. "Yes, Mom."

Bryn heated up the chicken soup she had made over the weekend, and then prepared a cup of hot chocolate. After Alex ate the soup and drank the hot chocolate, she had to admit they made her feel better.

"Now it's off to bed with you, Lex."

"I don't think I can sleep. My mind keeps going round and round. Whenever I close my eyes, I see Will struggling to breathe."

Bryn's heart went out to her friend. "You want me to stay?"

Alex smiled. "Would you?"

"I'd like to very much. But may I please borrow something to sleep in?"

"Sure. Let me see what I can find that won't totally dwarf you," Alex chuckled, finding humor in something for the first time that long day. "C'mon."

Bryn followed her to the bedroom. Alex disappeared into her huge closet, and came out a couple of minutes later. "Here. I think this will suit you."

Bryn's mouth fell open before wildly grinning. Alex held up a soft gray sweatshirt bearing the smiling likeness of Tigger.

"If you tell anyone, I'll simply deny it, Bryn." Alex smiled that charming, lopsided smile. "Besides, my little brother gave that to me and I can't part with it." A flicker of pain crossed her face.

"Oh. It's so cute." Bryn was delighted. "You're a Tigger fan?"

"Yes, but that's just between you and me, okay?"

"Okay." Bryn, suppressing a giggle, went into the bathroom to change. *Big, tough surgeon likes Tigger,* she smirked to herself. *Lex sure is full of surprises.*

Bryn brushed her teeth with the toothbrush she had borrowed from Alex the first evening she stayed over, and then finished washing up.

When she came out of the bathroom, Alex, looking exhausted and terribly sad, was already in bed. Bryn felt a sharp pang in her heart at the look on her friend's face. Then Alex saw Bryn in the over-sized sweatshirt and her whole face lit up.

"You," Alex said firmly, "look completely adorable."

Bryn blushed. "Thanks. I've always liked Tigger myself, but Eeyore's my favorite."

The nurse climbed into the huge bed and lay down next to the doctor. Alex, giving in to her need for Bryn's warmth, held out her arms and Bryn shyly snuggled into them. "Is it all right if I hold you?" Alex asked tentatively.

"Very all right, Lex. Do you think you can sleep

now?"

Alex shrugged. "Maybe..." There was a long pause. "Bryn, there's something we need to talk about."

Bryn tensed slightly. "Go ahead."

Chapter 7

"I...I think you can tell I've grown pretty attached to you over the past few days." Alex ran her fingers through Bryn's soft, golden hair.

Bryn's heart leapt into her throat. "I...guess so," she answered softly.

"And...I think you feel the same way about me. Am I right?"

"Yes," Bryn whispered hoarsely.

Alex sighed in relief. "Then there are some things about me that you need to know."

"Go on," Bryn encouraged, giving Alex a little squeeze.

Alex hesitated. "I'm carrying around a lot of emotional baggage...more than enough for both of us."

Bryn just listened, encouraging Alex with her body language.

"I haven't had a meaningful relationship with

anyone for a very long time." Alex closed her eyes. "It's...very hard to talk about."

"I'll be waiting when you're ready, Lex," Bryn whispered, gently stroking the surgeon's silky hair.

Alex sat up and wrung her hands together, her dark brows creased in pain. She bit her lip. "Bryn...I...I'm not capable of having a physical relationship right now." Alex stared down at her hands.

Bryn looked shocked and confused. "What...what exactly do you mean? You don't want that?" she asked, feeling a little hurt.

Alex smiled ruefully. "No. Nothing could be further from the truth. But...I can't."

Bryn struggled to understand. "Can you please explain?"

Alex was clearly miserable. "I...I can't."

"Go on, honey. It's okay." She rubbed the tall surgeon's back.

"I...I can give pleasure, but I can't receive it." Alex put her face in her hands as her stomach roiled.

It finally dawned on Bryn what Alex was struggling to tell her. "You mean you can't..."

Alex took a deep breath and nodded.

"Oh, Lex." Bryn gathered Alex into her arms and held her tight. "That must have been so hard for you to tell me."

Alex couldn't answer. At her emotional limit, she just held on to Bryn and let the warmth of her arms soothe her. The two women stayed like that for a long time before Bryn finally spoke. "Is this because of something that happened to you?"

Alex shrugged. "It isn't any one thing. It's more like a combination of things."

Bryn sighed. "Have you seen a professional about this? Maybe someone could help you, or refer you to someone who can."

Alex blushed, and then sighed. "Kate knows." Boy, does she know.

Bryn realized what Alex was telling her. "Oh." *I thought those two had a history.* The petite blonde scratched her nose.

"We went to med school together in Boston." Alex rubbed her temples. "She was the closest thing I ever had to a friend. She's been in Atlanta for a few years now, so I stayed with her while I looked for a place to live. Things were never really serious between us, and we parted friends. She tried to help me, even suggested seeing a colleague of hers. But...I just can't...it's too personal."

"It's not your fault, Lex." Bryn kissed the top of the dark head.

"If you want to bail out now, I'll understand," Alex replied quietly.

"No. We'll get through this. Together, okay?"

"Okay." Alex's voice cracked slightly, and she cleared her throat. "Are you sure?"

"Yes, I'm sure. We'll take things nice and slow, and when and if you're ready for a sexual relationship, I'll help you."

Alex pulled away and cupped Bryn's cheek in her hand. She slowly moved in closer until her lips gently touched Bryn's, and then she kissed her. Alex was unprepared for the surge of electricity that went through her. She had never experienced a kiss so tender or so sweet. It left her breathless.

Bryn thought she might faint from the intensity.

When their lips parted, she leaned in and returned the kiss, feeling as if she could kiss Alex's soft lips all night long.

Both women eventually pulled away, knowing things had to be taken slowly. They continued to tenderly hold one another. Alex spoke first. "These past few days have been like a roller coaster. I can't remember feeling so miserable, yet so wonderful at the same time." Alex kissed Bryn's cheek.

"I was just thinking the same thing." Bryn returned the kiss. "You must be exhausted by now, Lex. I want you to get some sleep. I'm worried about you."

"I really like the sound of that, Bryn." Alex patted her shoulder gently. "Put your head right here?"

Bryn snuggled into her shoulder, and they both fell asleep. Alex was free of her pain...for a while.

****

The little girl clung to her younger brother perched on her lap. She heard her mother whispering on the phone outside in the hallway, crying occasionally as she spoke. The youngster knew something was terribly wrong.

Her younger brother David sobbed quietly. His mother was acting strangely and wouldn't tell her two children what was wrong. He also knew if his brave older sister was upset that something was definitely not right.

Suddenly, the closet door opened. "Alexandra, David, you're going to Aunt Jane's house. Something has come up." She sniffled, but tried to put on a brave face.

"Mommy, what's wrong?" The little face was fearful, as huge blue eyes looked directly into her mother's hazel ones. "Something bad has happened, hasn't it?" The little lip trembled.

Her mother looked like a deer caught in headlights. "It's nothing to worry about right now, dear. You and David are going to spend the night with your cousins. Now come on."

The girl clutched her little brother's hand tightly. "No. I'm not going until you tell me. Where's my daddy? I want to call him." She valiantly fought back tears.

"You can't. Now let's go."

The two children were quickly hustled into the car and driven across town. The girl was so frightened that she thought she would be sick. She couldn't let that happen. Her mommy would be mad.

After hurried good-byes and a few perfunctory kisses, the children were sent to the playroom with their cousins. The girl sat quietly with her brother on her lap, hugging him close.

The girl's older cousin, a boy of eight, knelt down next to them.

"Please tell me what's wrong, Andrew? You can't keep it a secret from me. You're the only best friend I have left. Please." The girl looked pleadingly at her older cousin.

"Mom said not to tell." The boy was torn.

"You have to. I'll find out anyway."

The boy started crying. "Uncle David...your dad...he suddenly got real sick...and he...died."

The girl started screaming. The past week had

been a terrible trial for her. First, her best friend had left, and now, her dad was gone, too. Without the loving support of her remaining parent, she never recovered from the trauma.

****

Alex awoke in a cold sweat. Bryn still slept peacefully in her arms, and she hugged the petite blonde close, needing the comfort.

Is it really fair for you to get involved with Bryn? You're nothing but damaged goods, Alex. You can't even shed a few tears for the loss of your little patient. It's a miracle you have any feelings at all.

And what about being intimate with Bryn? How happy will she be when you're unable to let go with her...to give a part of yourself so precious in a relationship? How long can anyone's ego deal with that? I doubt yours could, Alex.

And what will Bryn think of you when she learns your ugly little secret? She'll have to know. Can she forgive you for that mistake?

You're not perfect, Alex. Just like Olivia said.

But Bryn is just too special to let go. You have to try. You already feel so much when she's around. She's awakened emotions in you that you thought were dead and buried. Besides, you'd never do anything to hurt her. Hell, you'd die first.

Alex kissed Bryn on the top of her head as her eyelids drooped. "Please hang in there, Squeak. I want to make this work for us," she whispered as sleep finally claimed her.

****

Morning came very early for the two friends. Alex had surgeries to perform, and Bryn was due at the hospital to work her seven to three shift. The alarm went off at 5:45 a.m. and Alex carefully shut it off. Turning her head, she gazed fondly at the sleepy, tousled blonde snuggled up next to her.

"Bryn, time to wake up." Alex shook her gently.

"Ahhhhh," Bryn squeaked as she stretched. Alex loved it when Bryn made that sound.

"Have you always squeaked like that, Bryn?" The tall surgeon grinned as she stood up slowly.

"Huh? What do you mean?" she asked, yawning and looking up with bleary green eyes.

"That squeaking noise you make when you wake up. You know, the one that earned you the name Squeak?" Alex tapped Bryn's nose fondly.

"Oh...that. Yeah, so I'm told...since I was tiny. Why?"

Alex chuckled. "No reason. It's just incredibly cute."

Bryn smiled sweetly. "I'm glad I can entertain you, Lex." She stretched once more, and then stood. "Well, I guess I had better go home and get ready for work."

"Would you like some coffee?" Alex asked.

"That sounds great. I can barely keep my eyes open."

"Same here. I'll just be a minute."

After making a quick trip to the bathroom to use the facilities and to wash her hands and face, Alex went to the kitchen to make coffee. Bryn got dressed and appeared in the kitchen, looking somewhat rumpled. To Alex, she was incredibly cute. "Here's your coffee, Bryn."

She took the coffee as Alex leaned over and gave her friend a gentle kiss on the cheek. "Thanks so much for coming over last night," she whispered in her ear. "It meant a lot to me."

"I couldn't let you be alone at a time like that." Bryn returned the kiss and gave Alex a warm hug.

"I'll see you at the hospital, Squeak."

"Good luck with your Tetralogy of Fallot patient."

"Thanks...I'll miss you." Alex stroked Bryn's soft cheek.

"Me, too. Bye, Lex." She gave Alex one last hug and was out the door.

****

Don't ya love her madly
Don't ya need her badly
Don't ya love her ways
Tell me what you say

Don't ya love her madly
Wanna be her daddy...

The huge operating suite was sterile and cold—literally. The room temperature had to be kept low because of the flammability of the general anesthetics used. The beeping of a heart monitor could be heard, as well as the hum of a heart-lung machine. In the background, Jim Morrison belted out "Love Her Madly."

"All right, take her off bypass," the tall surgeon commanded. She stepped back and sighed. Everyone held a collective breath as the tiny, newly repaired heart filled with blood, and gradually started to beat. Evidence of a smile appeared in the faint crinkle around Alexandra Morgan's crystal blue eyes.

"Close her up, Paul. I'll see her as soon as she gets to P.I.C.U." Dr. Morgan trusted Paul Silver implicitly to suture Emily Ford's tiny chest. She had instructed him in the art herself.

Dr. Morgan left the surgical suite; removing her gloves, cap, and mask as she did. Her long black hair fell across her shoulders, having been freed from the prison of the surgical cap. She went to the locker room and changed into her street clothes: a pair of denim Levis, a crisp, white oxford shirt, and black boots, adding a simple pair of 14k gold hoops to her ears. Her white doctor's jacket completed the outfit.

Alex was mentally and physically exhausted from twelve hours of nonstop work. She had performed two complex surgeries: one Coarctation of the Aorta, and one Tetralogy of Fallot repair, plus she still had to make rounds. And of course, Emily was waiting in Pediatric Intensive Care. Still haunted by the death of young Will Blake the day before, Alex was taking extra precautions with her latest patients.

What went wrong? she asked herself, as she made her rounds. *I can't believe I lost a patient to a common, routine surgery. I can just hear Olivia now. Don't be a surgeon, Alexandra. You're a woman. You'll never be as famous as your father, Alexandra. You don't apply yourself. I guess Olivia would really enjoy my latest shortcoming,* Alex thought grimly as she rubbed her temples and tried to think of something pleasant—Bryn.

Alex was looking forward to a home cooked dinner at Bryn's this evening. They had made plans earlier, when Alex saw Bryn in the P.I.C.U. The young nurse was caring for the surgeon's CoA patient after he was stable enough to leave recovery. The surgeon had no doubt that the boy was in very capable and loving hands.

****

The P.I.C.U. was awash with bright lights and sounds. A small blonde toddler lay in a sterile white crib. She was completely surrounded by tubes and machines, and a thin white bandage was taped to her chest. A short, dark haired woman was attending to her every need—and there were many.

Alex walked over to the crib to check on her little patient. "How's she doing, Claire?" the tall surgeon inquired.

"Emily's just fine, Dr. Morgan."

Alex stroked the baby's cheek. "I want to be notified immediately if there's the slightest problem, okay?"

"Certainly. She's doing really well so far, though."

"Things could change in a heartbeat," Alex said grimly as she walked out the door. "Feel better, little one," she whispered as she headed down the hall towards home.

Chapter 8

The petite blonde sighed as she prepared for her dinner guest. Changing into a pair of faded jeans, and a black tank top that showed off her perfect form, she wondered why she felt so melancholy. She was usually very upbeat.

She should be feeling on top of the world. The gorgeous Dr. Morgan was coming over for dinner. In addition, the tall surgeon seemed to be crazy about her. A smile flickered across her face. Bryn remembered their first meeting at the hospital.

She was caring for one of Dr. Morgan's post-op patients. As usual, she was telling the child one of her stories. When she had finished, she put on one of her favorite CD's, which she often used to soothe her patients. The gentle melody of "Never Alone" filled the room:

*Go to sleep,
Don't you weep,
Tomorrow's gonna be,
Tomorrow's gonna be,
Tomorrow's gonna be, a brand new day.*

Dr. Morgan smiled shyly from the doorway. "That's one of my favorite songs."

"Mine, too." Bryn returned the smile and inadvertently stared, unable to take her eyes off the magnificent woman in front of her.

"I'm Alexandra Morgan." The surgeon held out her slender hand to the nurse. When their hands clasped, Bryn felt a surge of warmth that went straight to her heart. This woman looks like a goddess, she thought.

"It's nice to meet you. I'm Bryn O'Neill."

Before Bryn could think, the surgeon had asked her out to lunch and she had readily accepted. Something special had happened between them that very first day. Everyone in the hospital knew that Dr. Morgan ordinarily avoided socializing with other staff members. Bryn was delighted to be the one exception to the beautiful doctor's rule.

As she French-braided her long, golden hair, she thought back to her arrival home that afternoon.

Her mom, Kathleen, had come over earlier to wallpaper her guest bathroom. The two were especially close and she often did favors for her elder daughter. As usual, she brought along the two family *dogs, Teddy and Gracie. The curious Welsh Corgis were ordinarily very well behaved—until today. Gracie had jumped up on Bryn's bed and decapitated her childhood stuffed dog, Noah.*

The damage seemed irreparable. Bryn was inwardly upset, but didn't make a fuss. She didn't want to make her mother feel any worse than she already did. Even when it hurt, Bryn put the feelings of others before her own.

In truth, she felt *terrible.* Noah had been with her throughout her illness, many painful and frightening tests, and finally, the heart surgery itself. She wondered at the strange twist of fate. Her own childhood ordeal of open-heart surgery and illness had been on her mind all day long. She could have died just as William Blake did. Bryn hadn't realized how fortunate she was until now. She had sailed through her surgery, rapidly growing into a healthy, active child.

Bryn sniffled. *I have to get out of this mood. I don't want to make Lex feel bad. God knows she has enough problems of her own. I know she's blaming herself for Will's death. She's so stoic and controlled, and such a perfectionist. No wonder she has trouble relating to others intimately. She seems to have an amazing capacity for love and tenderness for her young patients, though.*

As Bryn prepared dinner, her thoughts kept turning to how vulnerable Lex had looked the night before. *It broke her heart.* Right then she vowed to herself to stand by her beautiful friend—no matter the outcome of their relationship.

****

Alex didn't arrive home until nearly 7:00 p.m. Running on sheer adrenaline at that point, she decided to forego working out and headed straight for Bryn's instead. She missed the bubbly nurse and couldn't wait to see her.

After running a brush through her long, dark hair, applying blush and lip-gloss, and spritzing herself with Opium perfume, she felt ready to put the long day behind her. An enjoyable evening with Bryn was just what she needed. She hopped into her black BMW, and a short time later pulled into the driveway of Bryn's small but neat home. *Very nice,* Alex thought to herself.

Bryn opened the door before Alex could even ring the bell.

"Hi," Bryn greeted warmly. "Come on in."

"Thanks." Alex smiled shyly and stepped forward to lightly kiss Bryn on the lips. "I missed you," she said softly as she pulled away.

"I missed you, too, Lex." Bryn leaned forward and hugged the tall surgeon. "Um...why don't we go into the family room?" she suggested with a slight tremor in her voice.

They walked down a wide hall, which was adorned with family photos of Bryn with her sister and parents and, of course, the dogs. Alongside these were photographs of Bryn as a small child, posing alone and with another smiling young girl. In the younger pictures, Alex observed that Bryn was noticeably thinner, and very pale. The surgeon was puzzled, but decided not to comment.

"I really like these photos, Bryn," Alex complimented. "You were such a beautiful child, and you haven't changed one bit."

"Thanks, Lex." Bryn blushed. "They mean a lot to me." She pointed to a group shot. "In this picture are my dad, Kevin, my mom, Kathleen, and my little sister, Cameron. The two dogs are Teddy and Gracie. Gracie is, at this moment, on my bad dog list."

"Why?"

Bryn led Alex into her bedroom and picked up Noah's body and his head from the bed. "Look at this."

Alex felt an odd sense of déjà vu when she looked at the dog. Shaking her head to clear it, she replied, "Uh oh."

Bryn looked down forlornly at the pieces of a cherished part of her childhood. Unable to stop a surge of tears, she started crying.

"Hey. Don't cry...please?" Alex sat down on the bed and pulled Bryn onto her lap. Without thinking, she rocked the young woman, rubbing her back gently. "It's okay...maybe I can fix him. I am a surgeon, remember?" she crooned.

Unable to speak, Bryn just sobbed her heart out, burrowing into the warm, soft shoulder. Alex murmured soothing words into her ear, and continued to rub her back. Finally, her sobs quieted, and not a moment too soon for Alex, who couldn't bear to see her cry.

"What's going on, Squeak?" Alex pulled a tissue out of her back pocket and wiped Bryn's nose. "Tell me what's wrong."

Bryn told Alex everything about her heart defect,

about the surgery, her stuffed dog, the pain, and the endless tests. About how sad she was that Will Blake had died. And most importantly, how she had turned a difficult start in life into a career that she adored.

When she was done, the stoic surgeon was fighting back tears of her own. Clearing her throat, Alex decisively jumped up, grabbing the mangled dog and his head.

"Hold dinner for us, Squeak. I have an emergency surgery to perform." Alex quickly bounded out of the room, leaving a hopeful Bryn behind.

A half-hour later, Alex returned, holding Noah behind her back. With an endearing lopsided smile, she presented the beautifully repaired dog. Noah was now sporting a beautiful blue satin ribbon around his neck, expertly tied.

Bryn's mind staggered as the force of long buried memories resurfaced and overwhelmed her senses. "Oh my God," she gasped. "Lexi, it's you." She threw herself into Alex's arms.

"Of course, it's me, Bryn," Alex chuckled. "But why did you call me Lexi? I haven't been called that since I was a little girl."

Bryn hugged Alex, clutching the stuffed dog between them. "You're Lexi Morgan. Your dad performed my surgery. My parents took me to Boston because David Morgan was the best pediatric heart surgeon in the country. You made rounds with him one day, and we became friends. I remember when you tied a ribbon around Noah's neck for me...just like tonight. You tied it perfectly...even then." Bryn was so excited she could barely talk.

Alex looked confused. "I was just covering up

the suture line around his neck." Seeing that this was important to Bryn, she suggested, "Let's go sit down on the couch and talk."

Bryn, unable to contain her excitement, followed Alex to the couch. Once seated, the young nurse reached out and tucked a lock of dark hair behind the surgeon's ear. "Can't you remember? You brought Pinwheels to the hospital for me...because I wouldn't eat. You even brought peanut butter and blueberry jam sandwiches...all your favorite foods." Bryn chuckled. "I ate everything you brought. Heck, I'd probably have eaten Brussel Sprouts if you'd suggested them."

Alex wrinkled her nose. "Not a chance of that happening." She reached for Bryn's hand and held it.

"I had the biggest case of hero worship imaginable." Tears welled in Bryn's sparkling green eyes. "I cried all the way home on the plane."

Alex looked down at their clasped hands, crestfallen that she couldn't share in the memories. "I'm sorry, Bryn. I can't seem to remember." It felt like a piece of her heart was missing.

Bryn, always sensitive to other's feelings, suspected that something traumatic must have happened to Alex to affect her memory. "It's okay. Don't worry about it. I'm just so happy we're together again...we said we'd be best friends forever. I just can't believe you're here with me. And you sewed up Noah like new."

Alex smiled ruefully. "Yeah...I have many skills."

Bryn laughed. "That you do. You were probably sewing at the tender age of two." She wiped happy tears from her cheeks with the back of her hands.

"Three, actually," Alex quipped. "My dad had me pegged to be a surgeon by then." She paused, and then smiled sadly. "He was so funny. I had him wrapped around my little finger...there was nothing he could deny me." Alex's beautiful features grew dark.

"Where's your dad, now?" Bryn rubbed her arm soothingly.

Alex sighed. "He died of a brain hemorrhage when I was seven. An aneurysm in his brain suddenly burst." Alex fidgeted, clearly in pain. "It was totally unexpected."

"Oh, Lex. I'm so sorry." Bryn put an arm around her.

"My life kind of fell apart after that." Alex cleared her throat. "But I survived. I'm a big girl after all."

Are you, really? Bryn hugged her sympathetically. Alex looked like a little lost girl, so Bryn decided it was time for a dose of some much-needed TLC. "Listen, why don't we go into the kitchen and eat dinner? The lasagna's in the oven."

****

The two women walked into the cheery, open kitchen, decorated in shades of forest green and cream. Bryn opened the refrigerator and pulled out a bottle of White Zinfandel, impressing Alex with her uncorking skills. After the glasses were filled, Alex took hers and sipped it, then looked quizzically at Bryn.

"You never told me how Gracie managed to eat

your stuffed dog." It was a valiant attempt on the surgeon's part to be humorous.

"My mother came over to wallpaper my guest bathroom. Our dogs go everywhere with her." Bryn took a sip from her glass. "I suppose Gracie was mad that I wasn't at home, so she decided to get even. Mom's gonna love you forever for sewing him up, by the way. She felt responsible."

"I'm glad I could help out."

After setting the table, Bryn removed a green salad from the refrigerator. Next, she retrieved a loaf of garlic bread and a pan of lasagna from the oven, placing them both on the table. The two friends sat down to eat.

"Your mom must be really nice," Alex said quietly as she took a bite of salad.

"She's the best. Dad, too, once he figured out I wasn't going to break after my surgery. He was a little overprotective for a while there."

"I can hardly blame him. Plenty of my kids' parents are exactly the same way." Alex, still unsettled by Bryn's revelation and dredging up memories of her father, just picked at her food.

"Don't you like it?" Bryn asked, concerned.

"It's delicious. I'm just not very hungry tonight...sorry."

Bryn got up and stood behind Alex, wrapping her arms around the beautiful surgeon's neck.

"What was that for?" she asked.

"Nothing. You just looked like you could use a hug."

"You're a very perceptive woman, Bryn O'Neill."

Bryn kissed the top of the dark head. "C'mon,

let's skip dinner tonight and go directly to dessert. I think we both need it."

She led Alex into her family room and gently sat her down on a big, overstuffed, cream-colored couch, pushing a pillow behind the surgeon's back. "Now wait here while I get dessert and coffee. You look really beat."

"Will you stop fussing, Bryn?" Alex teased. "I always look beat after performing surgery all day."

"I know, but I just want to pamper you a little."

"You're really good at that, you know?" Alex gently tapped the blonde's nose. She loved the way it crinkled when Bryn smiled. Bryn winked and went to get dessert.

The tall surgeon sat back and closed her eyes. The last couple of days had been brutal. To make matters worse, Will Blake's parents had called, asking her to come to his memorial service on Saturday. Just thinking about it tied up the surgeon's stomach in knots.

Bryn quickly returned with a tray bearing two large slices of chocolate fudge cake and two mugs of coffee. "I bet you're hungry enough for fudge cake," the blonde teased.

That got a smile out of Alex. "Busted. I love chocolate cake."

"Me, too," Bryn enthused as she took a bite.

"Mmm, chocolate is just what I needed. It's such a mood elevator. Thanks, Bryn."

After coffee and dessert, both women cleared the dishes and retired to the back deck. A cool breeze blew the surgeon's dark bangs away from her forehead. Bryn thought she looked incredibly beautiful.

Alex sat down on a hanging swing, and encouraged Bryn to sit next to her, putting an arm around the petite blonde's shoulders. "Mmm, you smell nice. What are you wearing?"

"Red," she answered shyly. "You like it?"

"Mhm. It's nice on you." She gave Bryn a gentle caress.

"Thanks." Bryn nestled close, loving the soft strength that was uniquely Alex.

The tall surgeon impulsively pulled Bryn onto her lap. "There, that's better. You're so cuddly." She squeezed the blonde affectionately.

"Mmm." Bryn nuzzled her nose into the beautiful doctor's neck. "You smell great, too. That's Opium, isn't it?"

Alex nodded and let her body go into automatic pilot. She stroked the small blonde's back and they were quickly locked in a fierce embrace. Alex initiated a soft, lingering kiss, until her fears kicked in and she breathlessly moved away.

Bryn leaned in again, not wanting the contact to end. She kissed the tall surgeon deeply, and ran her hand up and down her friend's thigh. Alex moaned but carefully pulled back. "We...we have to stop, Bryn. I'm sorry." Alex stood up and leaned against the railing, trying to calm her wildly pounding heart with deep intakes of air. Her strong reaction actually caused her skin to pale, and beads of sweat popped out on her forehead.

"Lex, honey, are you okay?" Bryn came up to her and gently rubbed her back.

"Yes...No, not really...I just...I'm really sorry."

"It's okay. There's no hurry," she whispered.

"But I want to...and I can't...I'm too afraid." Alex bowed her head and covered her face with her hand, wanting desperately to fight her paralyzing fear of intimacy.

"Give it some time, Lex. I'm willing to." Bryn tenderly stroked the long, silky hair.

Alex wanted to drown in Bryn's loving touch. Much to her surprise, it spread a calming salve over her anxieties. Turning around, the grateful surgeon hugged the petite blonde tight. "You're so good for me, Bryn O'Neill."

"I hope so. Are you okay now?" she asked softly.

"Yeah. Just a little embarrassed."

"Don't be." Bryn rubbed the surgeon's back. "And if you want to talk about it, just let me know. It might help."

"I wish I could. I've always been taught to hold my feelings in, so it's really hard for me."

"I guess that helps you in your professional life...the stoic, controlled surgeon."

"Yeah...but it's murder on my personal life." Alex looked down and bit her lip.

Bryn gently took Alex by the shoulders and looked directly into her crystal blue eyes. "Let me in when you're vulnerable, Lex. I won't expect you to be perfect and I won't judge you. I can see the soft and beautiful soul you have underneath that tough shell...and I want to see more."

The surgeon smiled ruefully. "For you, I'll try." Alex gently cupped Bryn's cheek. *She's such an angel.* Swallowing hard, a cold fear gripped her gut. She was hit with the realization that she was falling in love with Bryn...hard. Never had she experienced such a feeling, and its intensity frightened her. "Bryn...you know I..." Alex swallowed hard, struggling to get the words out. "We...even though I can't...I can still please you, if you want...and, I'd like that."

As she watched the beautiful woman struggle, Bryn felt her heart breaking. She was unable to imagine what Alex was going through. *What happened to cripple you so emotionally?* She wanted to strangle the person or persons responsible.

"Listen." She took the surgeon's hand and kissed her knuckles. "I won't try to deny how attracted I am to you, but this relationship involves the two of us. I'm waiting for you, Alexandra Morgan...understand?"

Alex smiled. "I understand. Just remember my offer."

Bryn nodded as they both sat down on the swing together to cuddle. "Can I ask you something? Don't answer if you feel uncomfortable."

Alex nodded shyly.

"Can you..." Bryn blushed. *God, this is hard.* "Are you able to...feel pleasure at all?"

It was Alex's turn to blush. She paused, and then cleared her throat. "Yes...when I'm alone," she whispered hoarsely, wringing her hands.

"I'm sorry. I shouldn't have asked you that." Bryn felt like kicking herself.

"No, it's all right. It's a very valid question. Physically, everything works just fine. I have very intense feelings for you...at this very moment, in fact. It's just...emotionally, I have a problem." Alex ran her fingers through her long locks. "You could spend hours trying. I'm sure it would feel sensational...but...I'd never get to my destination." Alex bowed her head.

The waves of pain radiating off her friend felt like a knife twisting through Bryn's own heart. Gently kissing the surgeon's cheek, she whispered in her ear. "Let's talk about something else, okay? Everything will work out fine. You'll see."

An emotionally spent Alex nodded and laid her head on Bryn's shoulder. The petite blonde hugged her, and stroked her hair. After about ten minutes, Alex spoke. "I have to attend Will Blake's memorial service on Saturday. Will you take a rain check on that Braves game?"

"Actually, his parents asked me, too, since I cared for him that first day. I didn't bring it up because of everything else that's been going on. We can go together...give each other moral support...and of course, I'll take a rain check. We can go to the game another time."

"I'm so relieved that you're going with me. It'll make things a little easier." Alex squeezed her hand.

"That's what best friends are for."

Chapter 9

    The week was over all too soon for Alex as she reluctantly faced Saturday morning. The only bright spot of the day was that Bryn had come over early so they could spend some time together. The surgeon had been working late every night, and the two hadn't seen each other as often as they would have liked.

    The truth was, Alex was taking more time with her patients, giving them all that she possibly could. The extra effort was taking its toll on the beautiful surgeon.

    Bryn noticed that she looked tired and drained. She also seemed distracted and more irritable than usual. Dressed in a black, sleeveless linen shift, with matching pumps, and wearing her long hair down, Alex looked spectacular in spite of her fatigue.

    Bryn wore a simple black shift with black pumps. The sleeveless dress accentuated her sculpted, muscular arms. Always making her health a top priority, she was in excellent physical condition from years of working out. The two women together presented a stunning pair.

They were spending the morning on the screened in porch sharing a pot of coffee and talking about visiting the stables when the phone rang.

"Who in hell is that?" Alex grumbled as she answered the phone. "David?" Alex was incredulous. "You do realize it's eight o'clock on a Saturday morning...I was at the hospital, of course...I left a forwarding address, she can send my stuff there..." The tall surgeon's tanned coloring drained from her face as anger hardened her features. "Well, you can tell Olivia I said she can go fuck herself. I'm sure no one else would want to!" Alex slammed down the phone, shaking.

Bryn was aghast. She had never heard her friend be so rude to anyone. Before she could say anything, Alex rushed out to the back deck.

Bryn hurried after her. She found Alex leaning against the railing of the deck, trying to compose herself.

"Hey." Bryn put an arm around the shaking woman. "Want to talk about it?"

"I really don't need this right now." Alex drew in a long shuddering breath.

"Need what, Lex?"

"Family problems. I thought Olivia and David were out of my life for good." She sighed. "I don't even know how he got my number." She rubbed her temples, grimacing slightly.

"Anything I can do to help?"

"You're helping just by being here with me." Alex smiled ruefully. "I'll tell you about it another time. First I just need to get through the memorial service." She put an arm around Bryn. "Um...I'm sorry about my foul mouth." The surgeon looked sheepish.

"Don't worry about it. Just remind me not to get on your bad side," Bryn chuckled.

"That will never happen, Squeak." Alex hugged the petite blonde as they headed out the door to Bryn's jeep.

****

The memorial service was held at St. Luke's Episcopal Church in Atlanta. The ordeal was trying for both women, but much more so for Alex. To make matters worse, they didn't hold or comfort each other, preferring to be discreet about their relationship. Bryn was the stronger of the two by far, yet she cried quietly through most of the service. Alex, managing to stay in control as usual, tried to offer support to Bryn with sad blue eyes.

The tall, slender seven-year-old took her mother's gloved right hand. Her brother David held the other one as they moved to the front of the church. People were crying, and dressed all in black. Beautiful flowers were everywhere, and at the front of the church, was a casket. She told herself that her dad really couldn't be in there. He couldn't have died because he was never sick. How could a person who wasn't even sick, die?

But somehow he was. Her dad was gone, and they were going to put him in the ground and cover him with dirt. The girl shivered at the thought, and quietly cried.

Her mother scolded her. "Alexandra, you must be brave. Now be a big girl for Mother and don't cry. You don't want to make David cry, now do you?"

The girl bit her lip and shook her head. "No," she hiccupped, quickly drying her eyes.

The surgeon snapped out of her reverie, hearing Will's parents crying. *Be brave, Alexandra. Now you really are a big girl.*

The vicar delivered the small boy's eulogy. It was brief, as Will Blake had only been on earth for two short years. Knowing that Alex felt responsible for the young boy's death, Bryn looked at the surgeon, wanting to offer some solace.

"Are you okay?" she whispered as the service finally ended.

"I'll be all right," Alex lied. "I just need to get home as soon as possible." Bryn detected a slight tremor in her voice.

"C'mon, then. I'll take you home." Both needing the solace of each other, they left as quickly and unobtrusively as possible.

After they climbed into Bryn's maroon Jeep Grand Cherokee, the blonde pulled out a tissue and gently blew her nose. She looked over at Alex to see how she was holding up. "Hey." She cupped Alex's pale cheek in one hand, alarmed. "Are you sure you're going to be okay?"

The surgeon was pale and trembling. Sweat was

beading on her forehead. "I...I feel kind of queasy, Bryn. I just really need to get home...please?" she added with a touch of urgency to her voice.

"Okay. Hang on, I'll have you there in a jiffy." Bryn cast a worried glance towards her friend, who was growing more pallid by the second.

The moment Bryn pulled into the driveway, Alex jumped out of the car, hurried into the house, and just made it to the bathroom before she threw up. Realizing that Alex was sick, Bryn hurried after her. Her heart sank as she stepped into the bathroom. Alex was on her knees, retching violently into the toilet. The young nurse immediately grabbed a washcloth, wet it, and knelt beside the miserable surgeon. Bryn alternated between holding onto Alex, gently wiping her face with the cloth and rubbing her back. She never left her side until the spasms subsided, and Alex weakly tried to stand.

"C'mon, Lex, let me help you." Bryn guided the tall woman to the sink so she could rinse her mouth and wash her face before helping her to bed. After pulling back the covers, she found a soft, white V-neck tee from Alex's drawer. Alex was too weak to protest being undressed and assisted in putting the shirt on.

"There. Lie down." Bryn tucked Alex in and knelt by the bed, gently stroking her hair. "Feel better now?"

The pallid face was in stark contrast to Alex's dark hair. "A little," she replied shakily.

Bryn felt her forehead. "No fever, in fact you're cold and clammy. Was it an emotional reaction?" she continued as she absently stroked Alex's hair.

Alex closed her eyes. After a long pause she answered. "Not exactly...it's a really bad migraine that came on very suddenly...made me terribly nauseated."

"Why didn't you tell me?" Bryn asked gently. "We could have come home."

"It was very sudden. Bryn, it...it happened because I was holding all my emotions inside. It's...happened before."

Bryn's heart went out to Alex. Without hesitation, she took off her shoes and climbed into bed with her. Taking Alex into her arms, she stroked her hair. "Do you want to take something for the headache?" Bryn asked, as she massaged Alex's throbbing temples.

Alex nodded. "In the medicine chest...the same medicine you gave me last time...if it'll stay down...if it won't, you'll need to page Kate."

Bryn became alarmed. If the stoic surgeon mentioned calling Kate, then she had to be very sick. Hurrying to retrieve the pills, along with a small glass of ginger ale, she administered the medication, and crossed her fingers. After about ten minutes of stroking the surgeon's forehead, Alex fell asleep.

Bryn searched Alex's closet and found the Tigger sweatshirt. She changed into it, and then climbed back into bed with her friend, who was now sleeping peacefully. Sighing, she pulled Alex into her arms again. "Everything's going to be okay," she whispered, kissing a pale cheek. "I love you, Lex...with all my heart."

Alex smiled in her sleep, a very sweet and contented smile.

****

Alex slept for most of the day. Bryn had been up for hours and had changed into the clothes she had in the car: jeans, a form fitting pale blue tee, and sneakers. In hopes that Alex would feel like eating when she awoke, Bryn busied herself around the house, making iced tea, chicken salad, and lemon muffins.

By 4:30, Bryn was growing restless. Every half-hour, she peeked into the surgeon's room to make sure she was all right. Each time she checked, Alex was still sleeping soundly. *I hope she's okay,* Bryn worried.

Deciding to brew a fresh pot of coffee, she thought about the difficult day the two friends had just been through together. Alex had obviously been very upset by the morning phone call. That had been a bad beginning to a day that included a funeral for a two-year-old. Her friend was carrying around a lot of deep pain and anger inside, and Bryn wondered how she could help her release it. She feared for Alex's health if something wasn't done soon.

When the coffee was ready, she poured herself a latte-sized cup of the fragrant brew, yawning as she did. Then she took the steaming beverage out to Alex's screened in porch to drink it. The room was beautiful, decorated in deep blue and white. It quickly became their favorite place to relax with its wonderful view of the surgeon's private, wooded back yard. Bryn couldn't believe how close they had grown over the past weeks and how much they seemed to revel in each other's company. The minute Bryn realized who Alex was; she knew that she was in love with her. *Oh, face it, Bryn. You were in love with her before then. You feel whole when you're with her. All you want to do is hold her, make her happy, be with her...emotionally and physically. Oh, how you want to be with her physically. C'mon now, Bryn. You can do this. Just take deep breaths. You can and will wait...for Lex. Hell, you'll wait forever if necessary.* Bryn picked up a Pediatric Cardiology journal from the coffee table, and fanned herself briskly.

There are other, more important issues here, Bryn. For instance, will Lex ever remember our time together? She desperately wanted Alex to share that special memory with her.

****

Bryn had been moved to a private room several days after her surgery, and all the tubes and wires had been removed. The child was making a remarkable recovery, but the nurses had a difficult time coaxing her to eat. The tiny girl had few reserves to begin with, and she needed fuel to help heal her incision.

Around lunchtime, her new friend, carrying a large picnic basket, arrived for a visit. Lexi was wearing jeans and a pale blue Snoopy tee shirt, her beautiful black hair tied back in a loose ponytail. The little blonde couldn't believe that this big second grader wanted to be her friend.

The dark haired girl beamed as she hopped up on the bed and gave the slight four-year-old a gentle hug and a somewhat sloppy kiss on the cheek. "I didn't hurt your incision, did I?" the precocious child lisped.

The little blonde pulled her pajama top all the way up, peering curiously at the bandage. "You mean where your dad unzipped me?"

The older girl giggled. "Yeah, where Dad unzipped you."

The blonde tot sighed. "No Lexi, it doesn't hurt much. But I don't like the food...it tastes yucky." A lower lip poked out.

"I knew you wouldn't like it," she announced confidently. "So our housekeeper, Anna, and I made a picnic for us. Even Davy, my little brother, will eat this stuff. He's four, too." The girl reached inside the basket and took out a variety of goodies: peanut butter and blueberry jam sandwiches, chocolate Pinwheel cookies, little containers of apple juice, and a big bag of Cheetos.

The little blonde's green eyes grew wide. "Pinwheels," she squealed. "That's my favorite cookie."

"Mine, too, Bryn. Now eat up so you can get better." The older girl handed a sandwich to her little companion as she took a healthy bite of her own.

The child impulsively threw her thin arms around her friend and hugged her. "I love you, Lexi," she said matter-of-factly. "You're my best friend in the whole world."

"I love you, too, Bryn."

By the time she was discharged from the hospital, the girl had blossomed into a healthy, active little dynamo, with pink, round cheeks.

****

The petite nurse wiped tears from her cheeks angrily. "Why can't you remember, Lex?" Bryn stood up and paced around the porch. "How am I going to help you?" *I'm not giving up,* she thought. *I'll never let you out of my sight again, Alexandra Morgan...I know you're my soul mate.*

Chapter 10

Around 5:30, Bryn tiptoed into Alex's bedroom to check on her again. The dark haired beauty was just stirring. Sleepy blue eyes tried to focus as Bryn leaned over the bed.

"Hey. How are you feeling?" The blonde sat down and stroked dark bangs out of the surgeon's eyes.

Alex blinked sleepily. "Mmm..." she stretched, "very sleepy."

"You want to go back to sleep?" Bryn leaned over and gently kissed Alex's cheek.

"Right now all I want to do is hold you." Alex took Bryn in her arms and held her close. "You feel so good." She inhaled the sweet scent of the blonde. "Thanks for being here for me today," she whispered.

"I wouldn't want to be anywhere else." Bryn laid her head on the beautiful doctor's shoulder.

After about ten minutes, Alex pulled away.

"Sorry, but I have to get up...be right back." When Alex returned from the bathroom, Bryn couldn't help but notice that her elegant face was still pale, and her dark hair tousled.

"Lie down, Lex. I'll bring you a glass of iced tea."

Alex, still drowsy from the medication, snuggled back into the covers, relishing the feel of the soft sheets.

"Here." Bryn put a straw to Alex's lips.

"Mmm...that tastes great. Thanks."

"I also made chicken salad and lemon muffins if you're hungry."

"So that's what smells so good. Maybe later when I'm more awake." Alex paused. "I'm really sorry I slept all day."

"Please don't apologize, you needed it. I felt so bad for you."

"It was pretty rough. There's nothing worse than throwing up when your head is about to explode."

"Poor baby," Bryn crooned.

Alex smiled. "I'll be fine. Only my pride is hurt...I guess I didn't handle the memorial service real well, did I?"

"No, but only because you have to be so stoic and controlled all the time. You'd have been much better off if you'd cried."

"It's just not my way," she confided tersely, trying not to be annoyed with Bryn's observation.

"Oh, so throwing your guts up is your way," Bryn replied, her green eyes flashing with anger.

The jibe wounded Alex in her most vulnerable place. "I certainly didn't intend for it to be. I was upset...I held it in...I got a headache." The beautiful surgeon sighed deeply and closed her eyes. "You know, Bryn, I warned you that I was carrying around a lot of emotional baggage."

"God, Lex, I'm so sorry. I didn't mean it that way." She rubbed her friend's back soothingly. "I was worried about you, damn it. You scared the hell out of me."

"Bryn...let's be frank...I'm not sure if you can handle a relationship with me. Outwardly, I'm very much in control...especially at work. But you can see that my personal life's a mess." She ran her fingers through her rumpled black locks. "Until this morning, I hadn't spoken with a family member in years. And you already know the sad story about my intimacy problems. It might be best for you to back out now."

Bryn could see that Alex was teetering on the verge of tears. And she knew that all this was coming from the surgeon's deep insecurities. "Let's get something straight, Lex. I have absolutely no intention of backing out now. I already care too much about you. I only want to make you happy...to see you smile...you have the nicest one I've ever seen."

Bryn was really chipping away at the iron walls surrounding the dark haired beauty. Alex felt them slowly crumbling around her. "I care about you, too, Bryn," she replied, barely above a whisper.

"Then please trust me. Trust me not to hurt you, or betray you, or to think less of you because you're human...because you feel."

"I'm trying...but, it's really hard for me."

Bryn saw Alex's bottom lip quiver for just an

instant. She took the surgeon into her arms and held her close. The beautiful woman allowed it, unable to resist being held in those arms. She breathed in the scent of Bryn's fragrant golden hair. She felt the warmth of the small muscular arms. Most of all, she felt the love emanating from the heart of her best friend—a love that had already begun to mend a deep wound—inside her own heart.

Alex pulled away at last and spoke. "I think I'll get cleaned up and we can go out to sit on the screened in porch. Then we'll talk...I'll tell you about that phone call this morning."

Bryn was surprised but pleased that Alex felt comfortable enough to open up to her. "I'll make a fresh pot of coffee," Bryn offered, heading for the kitchen.

While Bryn brewed a fresh pot of coffee, Alex freshened up and carefully brushed her dark hair. She put on a pair of denim shorts, which accentuated her long, beautiful legs, adding a bracelet to her slender ankle. Since she often went barefoot, her jewelry box was filled with the bracelets. Alex preferred simple but elegant jewelry.

As Bryn brought out a tray with their coffee, Alex sat down on the blue and white loveseat, crossing her long legs as she did. Bryn tried unsuccessfully not to gawk, causing Alex to smile knowingly. She got a huge kick out of Bryn looking at her legs, and for a moment her troubles were forgotten.

"Um...sorry...I've never seen you in tight shorts before." The blonde cleared her throat as she sat down beside Alex. *God, I love those legs. Oh, how I would love to...*

"Don't apologize. I like you looking at me that way." Alex gave Bryn a heart warming, sexy smile.

Her hands shaking a little, Bryn poured coffee into two latte mugs.

"It's really okay, Squeak. You know, you never fail to make me smile." Alex took the trembling hand and tenderly kissed every knuckle.

Bryn slowly moved closer to Alex until their lips brushed tenderly. It was a gentle yet passionate kiss. Meant to affirm the deep bond forming between them, yet non-threatening to the insecure surgeon. "I hope I never do...I love to see that smile."

"Will you stay with me tonight?" Alex asked, a hint of vulnerability in her voice.

Bryn giggled. "I packed a bag just in case." She paused for a long moment as she mustered up all her courage. "Let's have that talk now, okay?"

Alex looked down into her mug and sighed. "I guess it's time." She paused for several moments, taking a deep breath. "That was my younger brother, David, on the phone this morning. I haven't seen or spoken to him or Olivia in three years." Pain shadowed the beautiful features.

"Is Olivia your mother?" Bryn took the surgeon's slender hand.

"Yes, biologically. But she's never been a real mother to me," Alex replied bitterly. "Now David, that's another matter. He's always been her baby from day one, her little male heir. They always clicked. Just like Dad and me...we were kindred spirits." Alex's blue eyes deepened a shade.

"Go on, honey. I'm listening." Bryn tightened her hold on Alex's hand.

"After Dad died, Olivia became more remote and controlling than ever—even to David. Many times, I was his substitute mother. When he'd get frightened in the night, he'd climb into bed with me." Alex sighed. "Olivia didn't have a lot of patience with small children, so I had to grow up very fast. And because I was so tall for my age, and very precocious, she treated me like a little adult...which I wasn't." Alex's voice showed absolutely no hint of emotion.

"Olivia has always pulled David's strings. He's dependent on her, wants to please her all the time. And me...after a while I became very rebellious and did everything I could to displease her. She didn't think I was good enough to be a surgeon and tried to discourage me...big mistake on her part. I became more determined than ever."

Bryn, noticing the breeze getting cooler, covered them both with a soft afghan. She felt helpless and wanted to do everything in her power to comfort Alex. The pieces of the puzzle that was Dr. Morgan were fitting together.

"Olivia always expected me to be perfect, to never make a mistake. She wouldn't let me show my feelings, but worse than that, she wouldn't allow me to be a child." Bryn saw a flicker of pain in the deep blue eyes. "I began to hate her, and I always wished that she had died instead of Dad. That, of course, just made me feel guilty."

Bryn rubbed and kissed her companion's hand, which had grown cold.

"A few years ago, I did something totally unforgivable in Olivia's eyes. David agreed with her and took sides. I couldn't believe he could do that to me after all I had done for him...I suppose he just can't be his own person. She never gave him the chance." Alex's face twitched, and Bryn could tell she was working hard to hold her emotions in check.

"What did David want this morning?"

"Olivia is selling Dad's cottage on Cape Cod, and she wants me to come and get all my stuff. David tried to be friendly to me...he even acted contrite...but I can't be civil to anyone who is friendly to that bitch." The surgeon's face darkened with anger.

So that's why there are no pictures of her mother in her office. Who could blame her? I seem to have my work cut out for me...but I'd do anything in this world for Lex...anything. Bryn poured more coffee for her companion.

"I told David to have Olivia send me my stuff. She can certainly afford it. I'm never going back to that cottage again. It was never a home after Dad died anyway." Alex hung her head.

Bryn sensed that Alex had had enough emotional turmoil for one day. "I'm here for you, Lex," she whispered in her ear. "I can't believe anyone could treat a little girl as special as you were that way. Not to mention the wonderful human being you turned out to be. We'll be all right...together."

Alex smiled sadly and squeezed Bryn's hand. "Together. I like the sound of that."

****

Needing to be close after such an emotional day, the two women spent the entire evening in bed together, watching old movies and cuddling. They ate sandwiches and muffins from a tray, and shared popcorn and hot chocolate while learning new things about each other. For instance, Bryn couldn't believe it when she found out that the tough surgeon hated snakes with a passion. She learned that little tidbit when the movie *Deadly Predators* came on. And Alex discovered that Bryn was terrified of spiders while watching *Kingdom of the Spiders*. Much to Alex's delight, the petite blonde clung fearfully to her throughout the movie.

Finally, around 1:00 a.m., the two were yawning. Bryn's head was firmly planted on Alex's shoulder; the surgeon's arms wrapped around the blonde in a loving hug. Even their legs were intertwined.

Alex kissed the top of Bryn's head affectionately. "I guess we had better go to sleep now, Squeak. I'm beat."

"Me, too," she yawned. "Mmm, you make the best stuffed animal." She squeezed the surgeon tight.

Alex chuckled. "I'm happy to oblige." They fell peacefully asleep. In spite of the pain they'd gone through that day, each wondered if they'd ever felt this happy before.

Chapter 11

On Sunday, the two friends visited Apollo, and Alex actually persuaded Bryn to ride with her. She enjoyed the feel of the petite blonde in front of her as they rode. It felt like the most natural thing in the world.

Afterwards, they ate a picnic lunch of peanut butter and blueberry jam sandwiches, Pinwheels, apple juice, and Cheetos, all prepared by Bryn in an attempt to jog Alex's memory. Although the surgeon couldn't remember their time together as little girls, she loved that Bryn had fixed her favorite childhood treats.

As the two spent more time together, Alex gradually relaxed. She showed Bryn an open and playful side that no one at the hospital had ever seen. Bryn was delighted, but she still wondered what the surgeon had done to alienate her family—particularly her younger brother, since it was obvious that the relationship between mother and daughter was in tatters from the start. Not wanting to push her friend too far, she decided to let Alex bring the issue up, when and if she was ready.

When Alex returned to work on Monday, she continued to be vigilant about the care of her patients. She had always been a perfectionist, but now she was even more particular, and kept working later than usual. Bryn worried that the surgeon would be stricken with another one of her agonizing migraines. *If she does, I'm putting in a call to Kate,* the blonde nurse vowed stubbornly.

Finally, to Bryn's relief, Friday arrived. She knew the surgeon could now let down her guard a little, and she and Alex would make plans to spend the weekend together. But first, they had a long and grueling workday ahead of them.

****

Bryn adjusted the I.V. drip leading into the tiny hand of the infant girl. A respirator breathed for her, and she was totally dependent on the myriad of machines, tubes, and wires surrounding her. Dr. Morgan had worked for endless hours repairing the many heart defects the child was unfortunate enough to be born into the world with. Now it was Bryn's job to care for her. Alex had requested it, and since she was such a respected surgeon, the staff was happy to accommodate her.

As Bryn recorded the baby's vital signs, Dr. Morgan entered the room. After smiling warmly at the blonde nurse, she walked over to the infant's bed. "How are you doing little one?" she asked softly, while gently stroking the baby's head with one finger.

Bryn couldn't suppress a smile at the tenderness Alex displayed as she examined her patient. She found it irresistible. "She's holding her own. I just wish she had someone who cared about her," Bryn said wistfully. "I don't see how a mother can just give up her child like that...just because she wasn't born perfect."

Instantly, the dark haired surgeon's mood changed from that of gentle caregiver, to quietly furious. Her blue eyes darkened to purple, and her face turned white. "Did it ever occur to you that she might have a damned good reason?"

Bryn was shocked. She had never seen Alex this angry before; at least not with her. "Now, take it easy, Lex. I didn't mean to judge this baby's mother."

Alex took a deep breath and counted to ten. She was losing it, and her tiny patient depended on her to keep it together. "I'm sorry, Bryn. I'm just tired, I guess." She then focused all her attention on completing the examination.

Bryn swallowed hard. "It's all right...just forget about it." Truthfully, she was hurt and angry; but she didn't want her feelings to affect the care of her patient in any way.

After writing orders in the baby's chart, Alex returned her pen to her coat pocket. "I'll call you later, Bryn," she said quietly, as she walked out the door.

The petite nurse nodded and returned to her patient.

Shaken by the angry exchange with Bryn, Alex went straight to her office. She felt like kicking herself. Bryn had no way of knowing what she had been through. *Maybe it's time I told her,* the tall surgeon mused. *She'll have to know sooner or later.*

Alex poured herself a cup of strong, fragrant coffee from the white carafe in her office. Feeling depressed, she sat down at her desk and sighed. *What if she doesn't understand?* Alex thought miserably. *What if she thinks I'm a monster?* The mere thought of Bryn's disapproval made her stomach ache. Alex put her face in her hands and worked on regaining her composure.

At that moment, Bryn peeked in the open door of Dr. Morgan's office. "Hey. Are you okay?"

Alex quickly straightened up. "Would you like some coffee?" she asked, changing the subject.

"Well, sure, but you didn't answer my question."

Alex poured Bryn's coffee and fixed it exactly as she liked. "Close the door and sit down, please?"

Bryn's heart leapt into her throat. She did what Alex asked, and then gratefully reached for her coffee.

"I...I'm really sorry for snapping at you, Bryn. That was very unprofessional of me."

"Unprofessional? Is that it?" Sage green eyes flashed with anger.

"No." Alex was shaking. "There's more...I shouldn't have treated my best friend that way." The surgeon looked down into her cup as she bit her lip. "We need to talk," she said, very quietly.

Bryn could clearly see that Alex was in a great deal of pain. She reached across the desk and gently squeezed the surgeon's hand. "Anytime you want to talk, I'll always be here for you...you know that."

Alex nodded. "Why don't you come over after work? I'll order up a pizza for dinner—with everything on it."

"No anchovies, though." Bryn wrinkled her nose.

"No anchovies...you've got yourself a deal." Alex smiled shyly, feeling slightly better since Bryn's anger seemed to have vanished.

"Um...I've got to get back to my patient now, but I'll see you tonight."

"Thanks, Bryn. I'd give you a hug and a kiss, but I'd better not do it here."

"It's okay. That's probably a good idea."

"Bye." Alex brushed two fingers against her lips and turned them towards Bryn.

Bryn returned the gesture. "Bye, Lex."

As the door closed, a single tear rolled down Alex's cheek. Swallowing hard against the lump in her throat, she wasn't sure she could get through this evening...but she had to try. Bryn deserved an explanation.

****

As soon as Bryn got home from work, she took a quick bath and changed into jeans and a soft gray, long-sleeved tee. After French braiding her long, honey gold hair, she applied a touch of make-up and perfume. Dashing out to her jeep, she drove to Alex's home. She was anxious to see her friend. It was obvious the older woman was feeling distressed over the events of the past couple of weeks. Her patient's death and the family phone call were part of it, but Bryn was sure there was more to it than that. She hoped that Alex would be able to open up to her.

As Alex opened the door, Bryn couldn't help but notice that the dark haired surgeon looked stunning in a simple white tank top and white jeans. Her slender feet were bare, as usual.

"Hi. C'mon in." As soon as Bryn stepped inside, Alex closed the door and pulled her into a fierce hug. "So sorry," Alex whispered as she buried her face in Bryn's soft hair. "You still mad at me?" she asked, sounding more like a frightened child than a confident surgeon.

Bryn squeezed the tall woman tight. "I'm not mad, Lex," she answered softly. "You're really hard to stay angry at, you know that?"

Alex smiled ruefully. Cupping Bryn's face in her hands, she leaned down and tenderly kissed her lips. The kiss deepened and intensified, leaving them both quite breathless. "Um...would you like a glass of wine?" Alex asked, as the two women tried to regain their composure.

"Sure. I could use one right about now," Bryn answered, as she willed her wildly pounding heart to slow.

They went into the kitchen, where Alex poured two glasses of Merlot and handed one to Bryn. Alex paused, gathering together her courage. "Bryn...I want you to know I'd never intentionally hurt you." She took a sip of wine. "You have no idea how important you are to me." The petite blonde's wide green eyes stared intently into Alex's blue ones. "There's something I want to tell you." Alex fidgeted. "But before I do, you need to hear the truth about my past."

Bryn swallowed hard. "Go ahead...I'm listening."

"I...I'd feel more comfortable sitting on the porch."

Carrying their glasses, they moved to the open, cheery room. As they sat down beside each other, Alex downed her entire glass of wine, then took a deep breath and spoke. "After I explain, you might not ever want to see me again." The surgeon's soul felt vulnerable and exposed.

"There's no chance of that happening, so get that idea out of your head right now." Bryn took Alex's hand and kissed it.

Alex gathered up her courage and sighed. "Bryn...the reason I got so angry with you today was because I..." She stifled a sob. "I gave up a child of my own once." Alex covered her face with one hand. "Only, I killed my child. I had...I had an abortion." Her voice broke on the words, and the hand that Bryn held trembled.

Bryn's mouth fell open and she gasped. She then took the trembling hand and kissed it, intent on showing support and acceptance. As Alex valiantly fought back tears, Bryn could see how much the effort was draining her. It tore Bryn *apart*. She wished desperately that Alex could release her pain. But the stoic surgeon refused to cry, taking a few deep breaths, and then regaining her composure.

"You want to tell me about it, honey?"

Alex nodded.

"Before you go any further, I want you to know that nothing's changed between us."

Alex sighed in relief, her lower lip trembling. She took in a deep breath and began. "About three years ago, I was feeling lonely and empty, and frankly, in need of release. So I went out with a friend—a resident at the hospital. We both got really drunk, and we..." Alex bowed her head. "We ended up in bed together."

Bryn looked confused. "But I thought..."

"I...I hadn't admitted to myself that I was gay then, but obviously I was...I had been with more than a few women...but I just told myself I did it to spite Olivia." Alex laughed bitterly. "Ironically, she never even suspected."

"What about David?" the blonde asked sympathetically.

"Yeah...he always suspected...said it didn't matter one bit. I never did come clean with him, though...I told him I wasn't sure. I was afraid Olivia would find out."

"What happened with the abortion?" Bryn put a sympathetic arm around the broad shoulders. Her body language conveyed nothing but love and acceptance, giving Alex the courage to continue.

She looked down at her hands, one of which Bryn continued to hold. "I found out I was pregnant a month later. I confided in David, who told Olivia...without my permission." She pursed her lips together. "He meant well, but...Olivia went ballistic. She called me a slut and said that Dad would be so ashamed of me." The surgeon hung her head. "You can't imagine how much that hurt." Alex blinked back tears. "I told Olivia I hated her, and that my father would have loved and supported me no matter what. We had a terrible argument, and she ended up slapping me across the face. Then I told her I planned on having an abortion as soon as possible. She said she never wanted to see my face again. I told her that was fine, she was never a real mother to me anyway." Alex's voice grew flat and completely devoid of emotion. "Two days later, I went through with the procedure. I knew I could never be a mother...I had no role model." Alex clenched her jaw so tight it was shaking.

Close to tears, Bryn shut her eyes against the pain. Her heart was breaking for her friend. "What happened with David?" she whispered hoarsely.

"He was terribly upset...said I was wrong for not consulting with him first. He's very religious and wanted me to keep the baby. After that, we just drifted apart...although I suspect Olivia had something to do with us not reconciling."

The two sat together for a long time, just holding each other. Eventually, Alex spoke. "I...I feel so guilty. I can never save enough lives to make up for what I did. I'm supposed to preserve life, not take it. My entire professional life has been dedicated to that." Alex's dark brows furrowed in pain.

Bryn wrapped an afghan around Alex and gathered her into her arms. She rubbed her back soothingly. "That's a heavy load you're carrying around, Lex...even for your broad shoulders. Let me share it...please?"

Alex nodded silently and hugged Bryn tight.

"What's done is done. You can't keep beating yourself up all the time because you're human. Maybe you made a mistake...but it doesn't change how I feel about you."

Alex's heart felt as though it would burst. "Bryn,

there's just one last thing I have to tell you." There was a slight tremor in the surgeon's voice.

"Go ahead, honey."

"I'm in love with you."

Bryn's mouth fell open, and she started trembling. "Would...would you please repeat that?" she whispered.

"I'm in love with you." Alex took both of Bryn's hands in hers, kissing them. "I feel like...I've always loved you." Blue eyes searched green ones for reassurance.

Bryn fought back tears. "I love you, too." She was laughing and crying at the same time. "With all my heart, my Lex."

They fell into one another's arms, Alex smothering Bryn with gentle kisses and Bryn gently caressing the surgeon's hair and face. Both felt as if they might burst with happiness.

"You love me...I can't believe it," Alex whispered, as she gathered Bryn into another affectionate embrace. "I never thought I would be happy again...but I am."

"You'd better believe I love you back. You're worthy of all the love and happiness in the world, and I intend to give it to you. It doesn't matter what else happens to us as long as we're together. I'll be your family...your best friend...whatever you need me to be."

Alex had reached her emotional limit, so she just nodded as she sat and held Bryn in her arms. After a long missing peace finally enveloped Alex, she pulled away and looked into Bryn's eyes intently. "Dance with me?"

"My pleasure."

"Hang on for just one minute." Alex stood up and popped a disc into the CD player. She held out her arms to Bryn as "Never Alone" played.

Lay your head, down to bed,
and let your slumber sweep your cares away,
In your dreams, chase moonbeams,
all the way across the Milky Way.

Bryn smiled in delight. "Our favorite song." She put a hand over her mouth and fought back tears.

Alex smiled and held out her arms for Bryn. The blonde walked into them and they moved effortlessly together. The surgeon held her as close as possible, nuzzling her nose in the soft, golden hair. Bryn had her ear pressed against Alex's warm breast, and she could hear her heart beating. Neither ever wanted to let go of the other.

When the song ended, Alex whispered in Bryn's ear, "I love you, Bryn. I'll never get tired of telling you that." She gently kissed the young nurse's cheek.

"I'll never get tired of hearing it. And I love you...with all my heart."

They kissed again, very sweetly, yet a kiss that each poured all their love into. Alex felt as though every wall around her broken heart was crumbling— piece by piece. It frightened her immeasurably, but she had absolutely no control over it.

After long minutes of just holding one another, Bryn's stomach growled in protest. Alex laughed nervously. "I suppose I need to get better at remembering to feed you, Squeak. I forget that other people get hungry. I'll call for a pizza loaded with everything right away." The surgeon's own stomach rumbled once the weight of her burden had been lifted from her chest. She couldn't believe that Bryn still loved and accepted her...but somehow she did.

"Don't forget, no anchovies."

"Okay, no anchovies it is." Alex telephoned an order for a large pizza with everything, and went into the kitchen to search her pantry for chips and salsa. She quickly prepared a tray and added two bottles of Coors Lite.

Bryn's eyes lit up when Alex returned. "Yum. Chips and salsa."

"You like?" Alex raised a dark brow. "I couldn't let my best girl starve now, could I?"

"Nope." The blonde winked as she dug into the chips, while Alex opened a bottle of beer.

"Dr. Morgan. Are you trying to get me drunk?"

"Me?" Alex asked innocently. "Of course not. I just thought we deserved to kick back a little after the past couple of weeks."

Bryn grew serious. "What you told me tonight took a lot of courage...I'm really glad you trusted me enough to share it."

"Me, too. I haven't trusted anyone in a long time...and I didn't want anything standing in the way of our relationship. I feel...so much better. Thanks for understanding." Alex gave Bryn's braid a gentle tug.

Bryn leaned in and nibbled the surgeon's lower lip. Alex felt it all the way to her groin. "Oh," she whimpered breathlessly. She then pressed her warm lips to Bryn's and kissed her deeply. The two were heavily involved by the time the doorbell rang.

"Oh, damn," Alex cursed, pulling away reluctantly. "I'll be right back." She caught her breath and straightened her hair as she hurried to the front door.

Bryn just stood there, touching her lips, which were still tingling from Alex's sweet kisses. Then the petite blonde realized something—Lex hadn't panicked when the two got involved in one very intimate lip lock. *Maybe she forgot,* Bryn thought. *Or it could have been the alcohol we were drinking. Even so, I'd better be very tender with her...her heart's still so fragile.* The blonde sighed deeply.

Alex returned with the pizza then, smiling shyly. "Are you ready to eat?"

Bryn just smiled devilishly and nodded.

Alex raised an eyebrow, smirking. She poured more beer for them, and they sat side-by-side, feeding pizza to each other. Bryn hadn't seen Alex eat that much since the first time they had shared Chinese food together. It made her so happy to see her friend in such a relaxed, playful mood. Lex could be so much fun, and she was incredibly affectionate—at least to her.

The two eventually polished off half the pizza and two beers each. A fierce storm blew up outside, caused by an unusually warm front moving through the area. Before Bryn could even react, Alex pulled her onto her lap and hugged her close. "Don't worry, Squeak...I've got you," she soothed. "I know how much you hate storms."

The blonde nurse was too perplexed to be frightened. "How did you know that? I never told you I was afraid of storms."

"Sure you did. Otherwise, how would I know?"

"You must remember from when we were kids. One night at the hospital, there was a terrible storm, and you refused to leave me. I was so frightened...but you stayed to get me through it."

Chapter 12

Two little girls snuggled close in a hospital bed. The younger girl had her thin arms wrapped tightly around her older companion. The dark haired girl good naturedly ignored the chokehold around her neck.

"Take it easy, Bryn. We're safe here. This is my dad's hospital you know, and he would never let anything happen to me or any of his patients. Especially if the patient is his daughter's best friend." She smiled endearingly; her missing teeth making her look irresistible.

"But I hate storms." Bryn let go of the girl's neck long enough to reach for her stuffed dog, then hugged them both. "Mommy, I want Lexi to spend the night...please?"

"When the storm is over, Lexi will have to go home, sweetie. It's against the rules for her to stay. But when you get out of the hospital, Lexi is always welcome in our home. Maybe she can come for a week or two next summer—if it's okay with her mom and dad."

Both girls' eyes grew wide as they imagined spending all that time together. Bryn's mother walked over and enveloped them both in a loving hug. Lexi was quickly becoming like another daughter to her.

****

Alex's face fell. "I can't remember, Bryn...I'm sorry. I wish I could." She kissed the blonde's cheek.

"Don't worry, Lex. I know you will someday...at least you remembered that I hate storms." And, just as she had on that night so long ago, Bryn snuggled closer to her best friend.

"It should pass soon." Alex paused, gathering up her courage. "One thing I do remember is caring about you—from the first day I saw you in the hospital, I had very deep feelings for you. Then, after you spent the weekend caring for me, I...I couldn't sleep on the nights we spent apart."

Bryn was touched. She knew how difficult it must have been for her vulnerable friend to reveal this to her. "I hate going to bed without you, too. Let's not do that anymore."

Alex grinned crookedly. "Works for me. Did you by any chance pack a bag for tonight?"

"You know I did." Bryn gave the surgeon a playful smack on her behind.

"Ow." Alex faked a pout as she rubbed her backside.

"Oh, I didn't hit you that hard, you big baby." Alex continued to pout, sticking her lip out further.

Bryn chuckled, then tried to push the lip back in with her index finger. The surgeon captured the digit between her teeth and gave it a playful nip. Bryn yelped in surprise.

"Now who's the big baby?" Alex slowly moved closer until they were staring into each other's eyes. She felt Bryn's sweet breath on her face as their lips met, oh so tenderly. *I can't stop kissing her,* Alex thought. *Her lips are so sweet, so soft, and she smells so good.* "Mmm," the surgeon moaned breathlessly. "I think you had better not sit on my lap anymore—at least for a while."

Bryn gave Alex a sultry smile. "Whatever you want...I'm letting you go at your own speed. And whatever speed that is, is fine by me. I just want you to be comfortable." She tucked a lock of hair behind the surgeon's ear and kissed her on the cheek.

"My current speed is not nearly fast enough." Alex smiled ruefully, her playful mood darkening. "I'm just really...afraid of failure. I mean, if we got started...and I couldn't...I..." She swallowed hard. "It's very humiliating...not to mention frustrating."

"Maybe we shouldn't have had so much to drink. I think it made us both..." Bryn blushed. "You know," she whispered in Alex's ear.

"Oh yes, I know all right. And trust me, I was there before I drank a single drop of anything." Alex smiled sadly, then slowly started chuckling. She couldn't help it. The look on Bryn's sweet, innocent face plus the comment the blonde had made, which had surprised her, sent her into a fit of laughter. Soon she was literally rolling on the floor.

"What's the joke? You're laughing at me again.

Lex, stop."

"I can't believe you said that. This whole situation is unbearable, but you're still so cute and funny. Oh, my sides." Tears were rolling down Alex's cheeks.

"Well, I was too embarrassed to say it out loud, for heaven's sake." Finally, the laughter became contagious, and Bryn joined her companion on the floor—rolling and laughing with her. It wasn't long before the petite blonde realized that something was terribly wrong. Her companion had curled up into a fetal position on the floor and covered her face with her hands. She wasn't making a sound, but her broad shoulders had begun to shake violently. Bryn scrambled into a kneeling position directly in front of her friend. "What's wrong, Lex?" she asked frantically, gently pulling her hands away from her face.

The surgeon's beautiful face crumpled. "I...I...can't hold back any longer. I..." Alex sobbed in great heaving gulps.

Bryn pulled her gently into her arms. "Don't try. I've got you, baby. Shh," she whispered softly. "Just let it all out. Everything's gonna be just fine."

Releasing years of terrible pain and anger, the usually stoic Alex sobbed uncontrollably. It burst forth with violent strength. Bryn, tenderly stroking and kissing Alex's hair, rocked her as a mother would a child, helping her through the storm. "Just let it all out, baby," she crooned. "I love you."

Alex clung to Bryn as if her life depended on it. "Don't...let go...of me," she pleaded, sobbing.

"I won't, my love. I promise." Bryn planted another kiss on the damp forehead.

"Why can't...my own...mother...love me?" Alex cried harder as she burrowed into Bryn's warm shoulder.

"Shh, it's not your fault. You're the most lovable person I've ever known," she murmured. "Something just went wrong somewhere and it went wrong with Olivia. It had nothing to do with you. Just look how much your dad loved you...and he was a wonderful person," Bryn's sweet voice soothed.

"Oh God, Bryn. I...I can't stop." Alex wept, panicking at her lack of control.

"Then don't, honey." She pulled Alex closer. "Shh, it's okay. Just go ahead and cry. It'll make you feel so much better." She rubbed gentle circles on her friend's back.

Eventually, Alex cried herself to sleep on Bryn's shoulder. From time to time, she involuntarily hiccupped. The petite blonde had never seen anyone break down like that before, and it drained her emotionally. The outburst hadn't surprised her at all—the only thing that surprised her was how long it had taken Alex to fall apart.

Bryn plucked an afghan from the loveseat and covered them both with it. She then wiped her own tear-stained face and kissed the dark head. "Now maybe you can begin to heal. I love you, Lex." Soon, sleep claimed her, too.

****

The slender seven-year-old stood on a chair inside her mother's closet. She then maneuvered herself up and climbed onto the top shelf. Smiling, she reached for her prize...a tan, Mohair Steiff teddy bear named Harry. Her dad had given it to her on her second birthday, and she treasured it like no other toy. She had loved some of his fur off, but otherwise he was in splendid shape.

She carefully hopped down to the chair, and then put it back exactly as she had found it. Taking Harry, she stopped in front of a large chest of drawers. Opening it, the little girl carefully reached in and tenderly stroked the fabric inside. She plucked the soft tee shirt from the drawer, and took Harry and the shirt into the linen closet.

She cuddled Harry close while holding the soft shirt to her nose. It still held the distinctive scent of her beloved father, and it comforted her. Crying quietly, she did not want anyone to hear her. Of course, it wasn't long before her little brother barged in.

"What's wrong, Lexi?" he pouted. "Are you crying about Daddy and Bryn? And why won't Mommy let you talk to Bryn on the phone?"

"Go away, Davy," she sobbed. "I don't need anyone anymore, and I want to be alone. Besides, if Mom finds out I have Harry, she'll just put him away again. Now please go. No one's supposed to see me cry...I'm a big girl."

****

Alex thrashed against Bryn's shoulder. "Go away," she mumbled, obviously distressed.

"Shh," Bryn crooned. "It's only a bad dream." She rubbed Alex's back soothingly.

Just as the angry face of the young girl's mother

appeared to scold her, it changed into the sweet face of Bryn, who took her into her arms. "It's okay, Lex. I'm here...and I'll never leave again."

Alex smiled and completely relaxed against Bryn's shoulder, falling into a deep, restorative sleep.

****

Sometime during the night, Alex awakened. Feeling uncomfortable and stiff, she realized that her head was on Bryn's damp shoulder. The petite blonde's arms were still wrapped around the surgeon, keeping the promise she had made earlier. Alex nudged her gently.

"You can let go of me, Squeak," she whispered tenderly. "I'm okay now." She stroked Bryn's soft, golden hair.

"Hmm? Ahhhh." The blonde stretched and yawned.

Alex suppressed a chuckle at what she had begun to refer to as 'the Bryn noise.' "Let's go to bed. We'll be more comfortable there."

"Okay." Bryn allowed herself to be led into the bedroom. Alex grabbed the Tigger sweatshirt from the closet and handed it to her companion—she loved the way Bryn looked in it.

While the sleepy blonde changed, Alex went into the bathroom to wash her tear stained face. She gazed into the mirror, looking at her red and puffy blue eyes. *I can't believe you did that, Alex. You broke down and cried like a baby. You completely lost all control. It's not like I had a choice, though. I couldn't have stopped if my life had depended on it.*

Once Bryn brought down that last wall, the dam just burst.

In retrospect, it hadn't been such a bad thing. It had felt so good to let all those feelings out—while Bryn held her. They had been smothering her for a long time, and now she felt cleansed. Still, she was terribly embarrassed by her uncharacteristic lack of composure.

Alex brushed her teeth and added a pair of blue silk boxers to her white tank top. As she brushed her long, raven hair, Bryn came in.

The small blonde looked approvingly at the surgeon's attire. "Um...I just need to wash my face and brush my teeth," she stammered.

"Help yourself, love." Alex smiled and kissed Bryn on the nose. She felt closer to her than ever—in spite of her embarrassment. "I'll be waiting for you."

The blonde smiled sweetly. "Be right there." As Bryn washed her face and brushed her teeth, she replayed the events of the evening in her mind. Seeing Alex in that kind of pain had nearly broken her heart. Yet she knew it was necessary for any kind of healing. *Maybe she won't get those awful headaches as often now. And maybe we have a chance for a normal sexual relationship. God knows it would relieve a lot of my tension.*

After unbraiding and brushing her hair, Bryn climbed into bed with Alex. Although the surgeon appeared pale and tired, she seemed more relaxed and contented than before, the tension erased from her beautiful face.

"Hey. You look like you're feeling a lot better...I think getting everything off your chest must have helped." Bryn kissed Alex's forehead affectionately.

Alex blushed. "I do feel pretty good...but that's because a certain beautiful blonde professed her love for me." She playfully rubbed noses with Bryn.

"Oh, is that it? Well, it's true. I'm head over heels in love with you, Dr. Alexandra Morgan."

"Right back at ya," Alex purred as she rolled on top of Bryn and kissed her gently. When the kisses grew too passionate, Alex pulled away. "Bryn...please...I want to show you how much I love you. I need to, so much. We'll be okay as long as you let me lead." She kissed the blonde's neck and worked her way up to a soft ear. Bryn shuddered...she had never felt so alive with sensation. She wanted to say yes...with all her heart. But she wanted this to be mutual...she wanted them to share their love together.

"As much as I'd love for you to show me how you feel, I'd prefer to wait for you. We're in this together, Lex." Bryn paused as an idea occurred to her. "Why don't we just play things by ear—see where we go. I have no expectations of you whatsoever—we can just make each other feel good...and you can stop at any time...okay?"

"Okay," Alex answered huskily, as she nibbled the blonde's ear lobe.

"Oh," Bryn whispered, as she turned her head to give Alex greater access. The woman beside her smelled so good and felt so warm and soft up against her, that she hoped she would be able to control herself. Feeling Alex's nipples harden through the thin material of her tank top, she longed to caress them.

Alex made her way back to Bryn's soft lips and

kissed her deeply. *She's a fantastic kisser and an even better lover, I'll bet.* The two were so turned on, that it wasn't long before they were involuntarily rocking their hips against each other.

"Oh God, Bryn," Alex breathed, kissing the blonde's neck. "I've never wanted anything or anyone as much as I want you."

"Mmm...works for me." Bryn ran her hands up and down Alex's back, and thought of moving them lower. "Are...you doing okay?"

"Yes." Alex was still frightened, but she knew Bryn would never betray her trust.

"Can I...touch your breasts?"

Alex closed her eyes and smiled. "Yes," she answered breathlessly. Bryn slipped her hand underneath the surgeon's tank top and cupped her right breast in her hand, gently squeezing the nipple. "Oh, I love you touching me there." Alex arched her back in sheer pleasure.

"Can I take your top off?" the blonde asked, a gleam in her eyes.

For a minute, Bryn thought she saw a look of panic in the blue eyes, and then it disappeared. Alex nodded, smiling shyly.

"You're sure?"

"Damn sure. Take it off," Alex answered, impatient.

Bryn smiled as she peeled the clothing from the surgeon's slender form. Her mouth fell open at the sight...she had never seen such beauty.

Alex looked at her through eyelids that were half opened. "Go ahead...I know you want to." Bryn smirked, and lowered her golden head to a beautiful breast. She suckled her tenderly at first, then harder. "Ohhh...God, Bryn...you make me feel so good." Alex ran her fingers through Bryn's silky hair, and pulled her head closer. She had never been this aroused before, and her hips rocked again.

Bryn stopped her ministrations. "Honey, would you like me to go anywhere else?" she whispered.

Alex looked like a deer caught in headlights. "I want you to...so much...but I'm afraid." The surgeon's dark brows furrowed in pain.

"Listen," Bryn whispered in Alex's ear. "What if I hold you while you touch yourself? You might feel more comfortable being in control, and maybe then you can have an orgasm." She nibbled her soon to be lover's ear playfully. "It's okay, you know."

The mere thought of reaching a climax in Bryn's arms melted any embarrassment Alex might have felt. "Okay," she whispered breathlessly. "We can try...for a while. And...please, take your shirt off? I want to see you."

Bryn had her sweatshirt off in seconds. Alex couldn't take her eyes off the beautiful woman. The thin, white scar running down her chest did nothing to detract from her perfect body. Alex very tenderly ran her finger down the scar, causing the blonde to tremble. The surgeon then kissed it. "You're so beautiful, my Bryn. I love you."

"You don't mind my scar?"

"I love it because it's part of you...it helped make you the special, strong, compassionate person you are. And it makes me feel closer to you...because my dad healed you."

Tears welled up in Bryn's eyes as she took Alex in

her arms. Her past insecurities about her appearance disappeared, and her focus shifted to the gorgeous woman she was holding. "Can I?" She glanced down at the silk boxers.

"Go ahead," Alex sultrily responded.

The blonde carefully slipped the boxers off and marveled at Alex's slender, naked form. There were no words to adequately describe the stunning woman that lay beside her. "I won't touch you anywhere you don't want me to. Okay?"

"Okay. Just kiss me...please?"

The blonde kissed Alex as she held her. A small hand moved lower to knead a soft breast. The surgeon moaned deeply as her need rapidly rose. Bryn guided Alex's hand across her flat belly to where it was needed the most, and then moved away. Knowing fingers began their work...she was more than ready.

"Oh, God...feels so good...Oh, Bryn." The surgeon's eyes were closed in ecstasy. The blonde held her; kissing her lips, her neck, her breasts. From time to time she couldn't resist watching Alex's hand work its magic...wishing it was *her* hand.

Alex had never felt such intense need...Bryn was driving her crazy...and what they were doing was unbelievably exciting. She couldn't have held back if she had wanted to.

Bryn could tell that her love was getting close. Watching Alex writhing and moaning softly was incredible; it was easily the most erotic thing she had ever witnessed. Bryn whispered sweet nothings into her ear, helping her along.

Alex felt the delicious pressure build and build until it burst, and she simply shattered. "Oh God, Oh

God, Oh God, Oh God! Bryn!" Her hips left the bed and she shuddered violently again and again. Bryn held her close as the intense waves of pleasure slowly subsided. Alex was unable to move or speak.

"Easy, love. Just rest a minute." Bryn smothered her with gentle kisses and stroked the damp bangs away from Alex's forehead. As she looked into the beautiful blue eyes, she wasn't surprised to see tears. "You okay, baby?"

"I'm fine...it's just...overwhelming. That was the most incredible experience of my life, and I..." Alex pulled Bryn to her chest, burying her face in the golden hair. Silent tears fell freely as Bryn gently rubbed her back. "I...I've never experienced anything like that before...and I haven't been able to climax with anyone...under any circumstances...for more than three years. And even before then...it was never easy for me."

"I'm so happy for you, honey. I guess that means you enjoyed it," Bryn said playfully, as she hugged her lover tightly.

Alex smiled through her tears. "Oh, yes. Enjoyed is not the right word. And I feel so close to you." She tenderly kissed Bryn's hand. "Before, I was broken...and now, I feel like your love is putting me back together...piece by piece." She wiped tears from her eyes.

Bryn's beautiful face glowed with happiness. "I love you, Lex...I always have."

"I love you, Bryn. You're my angel." She slowly moved in for a tender kiss. "Now it's your turn," she said in a deep low tone. "I have to show you how I feel." Once again, their lips met in a deep, searing kiss. Alex rocked against her companion. She couldn't get close enough. Her lips moved down the blonde's neck to suckle a soft, round breast.

Bryn's eyes flew open. The sensation was incredible. Alex's mouth felt so warm and soft, and she definitely knew how to use it. "Ohhh." The blonde threw her head back. "Lex, please don't stop." She pushed against Alex, needing her touch as much as she needed to breathe. She was aroused to begin with...watching her love earlier had nearly sent her over the edge. "Lex, please...touch me."

Alex smiled her sexy, lop-sided smile. She loved seeing this side of Bryn. "You like that, huh? Show me what you want," she whispered in her ear.

Bryn boldly took the surgeon's hand and placed it on her gray cotton panties. "These are gonna have to go," Alex teased, removing them in one swift motion. Her throat went dry when she saw her love naked for the first time. Unprepared for the surge of emotion that raced through her body she stared at Bryn for a long moment.

"Lex," Bryn complained. "I showed you what I want. Please...don't stop."

Alex smiled as she moved her hand slowly down Bryn's flat belly, stopping at the moisture between her legs.

"Oh, Lex. Right there...yes." Bryn decided right away that Alex had the most talented hands on earth.

Suckling a soft breast, Alex moved her hand continuously below. From time to time, she would alternate breasts; then kiss her love's neck, lips, and ears.

Bryn felt like she was going to die. It was all she could do to keep from touching Alex where she wanted to touch her most—but she didn't want to rush her. She felt the pressure deep within her reach the boiling point. Lex was a fantastic lover—just as she had expected.

"Lex," she moaned softly. "I need you...I want you to..."

"You want me inside?" She kissed the blonde's ear, and then blew in it.

"Yes. Now."

Alex gently slipped two fingers inside, keeping up a steady motion, then carefully added another. She continued planting tender kisses and nips everywhere, focusing on her lover's beautiful breasts. It didn't take long.

Bryn suddenly held tight to Alex and stiffened. "Oh...Oh...Oh...Lex. Ohhh." Her release ripped through her...she shivered as she clung to her love. Finally, she collapsed limply in Alex's arms.

"Ah, Bryn...are you gonna be okay?" she teased.

"As long as we stay in this bed for the next two days," Bryn laughed breathlessly. "You are wonderful. It's never been like this for me before." Tears welled in the clear, green eyes.

Alex beamed. "For me either. I'm so glad I made you happy. That's all I ever want to do, you know." She kissed Bryn's nose as she held her close.

"I'm very happy, my Lex. I love you so much." She kissed her partner's soft, full lips.

Alex gently pulled back. "I love you, too...but don't start something you can't finish."

Bryn moved in for another kiss. "Oh, I intend to finish all right."

Chapter 13

Bryn cuddled close to her pensive companion, gently rubbing her broad shoulders. Alex's internal pain was palpable, and she longed to soothe it. "It's okay, honey," she whispered in her ear. "We can try again some other time."

The surgeon sighed deeply. "I'm really sorry, Bryn. You don't know how much."

"Don't you dare apologize...I didn't expect everything to just suddenly be perfect. You've still got a lot of pain inside that you haven't dealt with yet. Besides, we were able to share some wonderful moments anyway. Don't you agree?"

Alex smiled ruefully. "Yes. Wonderful isn't the word. I can't even imagine what it would be like if you really made love to me—I probably wouldn't be able to survive it," she chuckled.

Bryn's smile lit up the room. She was flattered that this beautiful, passionate woman was totally enamored of her. Even though Alex had panicked when Bryn attempted to take control of their lovemaking, they quickly switched gears, and Bryn did everything she could to intensify the pleasure Alex was feeling from touching herself. She went on to have another very powerful orgasm and then proceeded to make her blonde companion very happy—no less than three times. Bryn sighed. She was quickly becoming addicted to her gorgeous lover's charm.

"I've been meaning to tell you something, Lex." She kissed the back of the dark head as she cuddled up against the woman's broad back. "My mom and dad are dying to meet the famous Lexi Morgan—all grown up and a famous surgeon now."

Alex chuckled. "They remember me?"

"Are you kidding? They think you're some kind of saint. You were so good to me when I was sick; they just loved you. Mom said she would have taken you home in a heartbeat."

I wish she would have, the surgeon thought bitterly. "Do they know about us?"

Bryn blushed. "Well, they don't know about tonight." The petite blonde stifled a giggle. "But they know we've been seeing each other, and my parents have always known about my preferences. They seem ecstatic that I'm with you. Mom always said there was some kind of magical bond between us."

"I wish I could remember that." Alex looked at Bryn with sad blue eyes.

"You will...just give it some time. We can get through anything...together." She tenderly clasped hands with her love.

"I love you, Bryn," Alex whispered, her voice

cracking slightly.

"I love you, too, Lex." They fell into each other's arms as the sun came up.

****

"I'll be back as soon as I have lunch with Mom." The blonde finished brushing her teeth, and then threw on a soft, forest green turtleneck. She zipped up her jeans, and then donned a pair of black suede hiking boots.

Her companion was dressing to go to the hospital at the same time. Alex grumbled as she slipped into a pair of black dress slacks and a white silk shirt with flat, black pumps. She had always despised dressing up, even when she was tiny. "I hate these shoes," she complained irritably.

Bryn smiled as she brushed out her golden hair. "I was going to ask you what it is about you and shoes...what gives?"

Alex thought a minute. "Apparently, I began removing my shoes at a very young age. Olivia used to enjoy dressing me up like her little doll, which I hated. I had every color of Mary Janes they made." The surgeon smiled mischievously. "I guess Olivia hadn't counted on me being born with very advanced fine motor skills. My little fingers could unbuckle the most difficult straps...and they did. It used to really piss her off. That was the beginning of us butting heads."

The petite blonde grinned broadly. "I can just see you. You must have been so cute." She kissed Alex's perfect nose.

"I was a bit of a terror...always taking things apart. But our housekeeper thought I was a really sweet kid anyway, and she always catered to me. Of course, Dad thought I could do no wrong." Alex paused. "What were you like as a kid—after you got well?"

"I was into every sport imaginable and a real daredevil. I always had to prove to myself that I was healthy and normal, just like everyone else. I once played softball with a cast on my leg."

"That's my Squeak. You little spitfire." Alex gave Bryn a warm, heartfelt hug. "I'm gonna miss you like crazy today." The surgeon picked up her black bag. "If I'm not here when you get back, I'll be at the stables."

"Okay...I'll miss you, too, love." Bryn kissed Alex's soft lips tenderly, and then reluctantly pulled away. They had time for one more hug, and then they both went out the door.

****

"Mom. Over here." The petite blonde motioned to her mother to join her in the cozy booth of their favorite restaurant. She stood up and enveloped the attractive woman in a warm hug.

"Bryn, darling," her mother drawled. "You look wonderful. Are you in love?" The older woman could have easily been Bryn in twenty-five years they were so much alike. Except Kathleen O'Neill had lovely, shoulder length, auburn colored hair.

"Yes, Mom. I'm very much in love." Bryn blushed and then smiled broadly.

"With Lexi, I presume." Kathleen pushed her daughter's long hair off her shoulders in a motherly gesture.

"Yes, but I don't think she'll appreciate you calling her Lexi anymore. She's six feet tall now, and one of the most respected surgeons in the country. She goes by Alex, but I call her Lex." Bryn got a faraway look in her eyes.

"I'm so happy for you, sweetheart." She kissed her daughter on the cheek. "I've never seen you like this before."

"I've never felt this way before. The minute she walked into that hospital room, that was it for me. Then when I remembered who she was—the feelings intensified tenfold. I know she's my soul mate and I'm never letting her go."

"You know your father will be so happy. You've never been anything but a joy to us both, except when you were scaring us witless with your daredevil phase."

"Sorry about that," Bryn giggled, then paused. "Mom, I hate to change the subject, but I need to ask you something. It's very important."

"Go ahead, Bryn."

At that moment their waitress appeared. Bryn ordered a cheeseburger and fries; and Kathleen, a Caesar salad with grilled chicken.

"What can you tell me about Olivia Morgan?" Bryn took a sip of ice water and looked intently into her mother's eyes.

A similar pair of green eyes gazed back. "You know, Bryn, my memories of that time in the hospital are very vivid and I do remember a lot." She paused, deep in thought. "I know that she was very different from Dr. Morgan—he was not only a wonderful surgeon, he was also a very warm and loving individual. He completely doted on Lexi, and sometimes I wonder if her mother might have been jealous."

"Tell me more," Bryn, insatiably curious about her love's childhood, encouraged.

"Lexi's dad encouraged your friendship. Olivia, I think, didn't know what to make of it. She seemed remote and self-centered, and I never once saw her be affectionate towards her daughter. I never understood that—Lexi was the sweetest, most beautiful child. Plus, she was so confident and mature for her age. I think everyone loved her—although I'm not so sure about her mother." The older woman looked sadly at Bryn. "Once you left the hospital, I heard that Dr. Morgan had died suddenly. That must have completely devastated Lexi. Then, when we tried to keep in touch..." She paused, remembering her little girl crying, heartbroken. "Our calls and letters were always ignored."

Bryn winced. "Mom, Lex can't remember anything about our childhood friendship. I think something hurt her so much that she blocked things out...and I'm almost afraid to find out what it was. She's told me some awful things about her mother—she's estranged from both her mother and her younger brother. I know she's in a lot of pain and I have to help her somehow." Big tears welled in the clear green eyes.

Kathleen leaned over and hugged her daughter. "I'm sure you're already helping her just by loving her. You have the biggest heart in the world, you know?"

Bryn wiped tears from her eyes and sniffed. "Lex has a very big heart, too. Only hers is broken." She gratefully accepted a tissue from her mom. "In some ways, it's like she's emotionally crippled."

"I can tell how much you care for her, darling. She'll be okay...she has a lot going for her. And if she wants, she has a ready made family right here in town...Me, Dad, and Cam."

"Thanks, Mom." More tears fell, and the blonde bravely wiped them away. She took a deep breath. "I can do this...I can be strong for her. Until she's able to be strong for herself again. I know she has the heart of a hero in there...once it's mended, there'll be no stopping her."

****

Dr. Alex Morgan sat at her desk, her hand hovering over the phone. Taking a deep breath, she dialed a number, then hung up. "C'mon Alex," she told herself. "You're doing this for Bryn—have some balls and go ahead and do it. She's already helped you so much, but she can't solve all your problems—they're too deep. You should have remembered her by now—*unless you're afraid to.*" Trembling, she dialed again. Just as she was ready to hang up, a voice on the other end answered.

"This is Dr. Taylor."

"Kate, Alex here. I...I need some help." She fought down the bile rising in her throat. "I...Bryn and I...we're together now, and I can't do anything to jeopardize that. I love her more than anyone I've ever loved in my whole life...and I...need help." She rubbed her temples, which were starting to ache. "Will you give me a referral?"

Kate's heart went out to her stoic friend. "Sure...I think it's wonderful that you found Bryn...you need love as much as anyone else...even if you won't admit it." The doctor paused. "I know how difficult this must be—you obviously love her very much. She's a lucky woman."

"No...I'm the lucky one." Alex hastily scribbled down the name and number, thanked Kate, and then hung up. "Only for you, Bryn," she sighed. "Only for you."

****

Around four o'clock, Bryn pulled into Alex's driveway. She was delighted to see the shiny, black BMW parked in the garage. Bryn had missed Lex terribly, and all she wanted to do was hug her and breathe in her wonderful perfume. As soon as Bryn opened the door, her dark haired companion literally swept her off her feet. She picked the petite blonde up and sat down on the couch, holding her on her lap.

"I don't like to be away from you, Bryn O'Neill." Alex gave her a big bear hug.

"And I don't like to be away from you, Alexandra Morgan," she answered, as she kissed the dark bangs. "By the way, I think you have a beautiful name— what's the middle initial stand for?" She traced a finger across a dark brow.

"Do you really want to know?" Alex asked reluctantly.

"Yeees."

"Oh, all right. Since you told me yours. It's Devin."

"Ooo, I like that very much." She ran fingers through the soft, dark hair.

"Really?"

"Really." Full lips kissed their way across her lover's eyelids playfully.

"Bryn? Are you trying to seduce me?"

"Uh huh." The blonde giggled. "You haven't changed out of your dress clothes yet, and I thought I'd help you."

Alex chuckled. "You are so incorrigible. But I think I like it." She slipped the turtleneck over her companion's head, and put her very talented hands to good use.

Much later, after bathing together, Bryn got dressed and Alex changed into comfortable clothes—a pale blue turtleneck and black Levis. The petite blonde had delighted in brushing out her companion's beautiful hair, even though Alex had initially put up a fuss about it.

"Was that so bad now?" Bryn teased as she put the brush away.

"No," Alex admitted sheepishly. "Actually, it felt sensational."

"I told you it would." Bryn paused, swallowing hard. "I'm really thirsty, Lex. Do you have anymore of that Peach Snapple anywhere?"

"Not up here, but there's some in the fridge down in the basement. Want me to get one for you?"

"No, I can get it. Want anything while I'm down there?"

"Just a Coors Lite. I'll be out on the porch, reading my journal."

Bryn kissed her and then went downstairs. She opened the refrigerator and removed the two beverages. As she turned to head back up, something caught her eye. In the corner of the room, sat a beautiful, polished ebony, baby grand piano. Bryn imagined that it was a very expensive instrument. The mystery of it being in the basement captured her curiosity as she headed back upstairs.

"Lex, can I ask you something?" She handed her companion the beer and then sat next to her on the loveseat.

"I guess." Alex looked a little nervous.

"Why is that beautiful piano in your basement?" Bryn took a sip of her beverage.

Crystal blue eyes darkened. "I don't play anymore, that's all." A look of deep sadness crossed her beautiful features.

Nimble, slender fingers moved across the keyboard, producing a symphony of sounds. The beautiful, dark haired ten-year-old possessed talent far beyond her years.

"Alexandra. You missed a note. You haven't been practicing, have you? Practice makes perfect, Alexandra. You've probably been spending too much time with that useless horse of yours." Stern hazel eyes looked into emotionless blue ones.

"I'll practice harder, mother," she answered flatly. Then, under her breath, "Go fuck off, Olivia. I hate you."

Bryn waved her hand across Alex's glazed blue eyes. "Oh no, you don't. No keeping painful stuff to yourself anymore. I thought after last night, we were going to be open with each other."

Alex sighed. "You're right...I used to play...quite well. But Olivia used to push and push and nag and nag until I grew to hate it. I guarantee you that if I sat down to play right now I'd have a full-blown migraine in ten minutes. So that's why it's down there."

Bryn's eyes narrowed. *If I ever see this bitch, I'm gonna have to have to hurt her.* She took a deep breath and concentrated on lightening the mood a little. "I'm sorry I asked you about it, honey. I would have loved to hear you play, but not if it's going to make you sick."

"Don't worry...I don't blame you for asking." Alex took one of Bryn's hands and kissed it. "I want to tell you something while I still have the nerve."

"Okay," Bryn encouraged, rubbing her soul mate's back soothingly.

Alex groaned, leaning into the touch. "I asked Kate for a referral today...to see a therapist. I want to remember...and I want to be able to let you make love to me. What we've been doing is wonderful...but I need more." Her dark brows furrowed in pain. "*You*...need more. Will you please...go with me?"

Bryn's eyes filled with tears as she took Alex in her arms. "Yes...I'll go with you. We can do this...we can do anything. We're partners, right?"

A hint of a smile crossed Alex's face as she nodded. "You do realize that this won't be easy?" The dark haired surgeon gently pulled away, rubbing her aching temples with both hands.

"Yes...but you're certainly worth it. Here—let me do that." Bryn began a slow gentle, massage of her lover's temples. "You're not getting a migraine, are you?" Green eyes were filled with worry.

Alex sighed in relief at the gentle touch. "No, it's just tension. I...I'm just dreading this so much. It's...very humiliating. I hate exposing the most intimate part of my life to a complete stranger."

"I'll be there for you, honey," Bryn soothed. "Don't worry."

Alex gathered Bryn in her arms for a tender hug. "You're my angel, Bryn O'Neill...and the best thing that has ever happened to me."

"I feel exactly the same way about you, my beautiful Lex." She hugged her lover tightly. "And you're so cuddly, too."

Alex chuckled, raising an eyebrow. "Me? Cuddly?"

"Yes, you. Very cuddly." Bryn kissed the surgeon's nose and stood up. "I'm going to start dinner. Why don't you keep me company?"

Alex laughed outright. "Do you think I'd willingly be separated from you for a single moment? Besides, even though I'm a terrible cook, I'm sure there's something I can do to help out." The two made their way into the spacious, blue and white kitchen.

"You don't have to help. After all, you did my laundry for me. I really appreciate that by the way." The petite blonde pulled two steaks from the refrigerator.

"I really didn't mind. I actually enjoyed folding your cute little underwear." She tapped the blonde's nose playfully.

"Lex." Bryn feigned irritation, but failed miserably. The beautiful surgeon pulled her close for a warm, passionate kiss that made it difficult for Bryn to remain standing. When it was over, she just stood there, touching her still tingling lips.

"Mad at me?" Alex smirked.

"You know I can never be mad at you, my love." Bryn paused, playing with a lock of Alex's hair. "I have a feeling though that if I don't get back to cooking dinner soon, we aren't going to have any."

"You know, I think you could be right." Alex managed to tear herself away from Bryn, and pulled two baking potatoes from a bin. A half-hour later, steaks were grilled, potatoes microwaved, and salads made. The two women sat down to dinner out on the screened in porch.

"How were things at the hospital today?" Bryn asked between bites.

Alex took a sip of wine. "My transplant patient is doing great. Her prognosis is excellent." The surgeon tried to contain her excitement, but she wasn't fooling Bryn. The blonde knew how much Alex's patients meant to her. She was sure her career was what kept her together through all her difficulties.

"That's good news, but not surprising...considering who her doctor is." Bryn dug into her potato hungrily. "I'm so proud of you. Everyone else had given up on that little girl."

"You are so biased. And I definitely like it. But in my opinion, she's doing so well because she had the best nurse in the hospital caring for her post-op." Alex leaned over and kissed the blonde's soft cheek.

"You make me smile so much, I think my face is gonna crack."

"I love making you smile, Lex." Green eyes gazed into blue.

"We're really mushy today, aren't we?"

"Mhm. But I can't help it."

"Me either." Alex grinned crookedly. "So how was lunch with your mom?"

"Good. She's a real sweetheart. I just know you'd love her—and, well, she already loves you. After all, she loved you when you were Lexi, and I know she'll be crazy about you now. She and Dad can't wait to meet you." Bryn noticed the pained expression on Alex's face. Her pupils grew larger, and she swallowed audibly. "There it is again. What's wrong, honey?"

"There's what?"

"Your deer caught in headlights look." Bryn rubbed Alex's slender arm. She had trouble keeping her hands to herself when she was with the beautiful surgeon.

"I...I'm feeling a little anxious about seeing your parents again." Alex felt disgusted with herself. "No, that's not true, Bryn. I'm downright terrified."

Bryn looked puzzled. "But why?"

"I'm afraid..." Alex pushed her plate away, her stomach starting to ache. "I'm afraid to remember...and I don't know why. Logically, I want to remember...very much. But emotionally...I don't. Every time I even think about it, I get this terrible feeling of dread."

The petite blonde had a sinking feeling in the pit of her stomach as well. She stood up and enveloped her lover in a soothing hug, rubbing her hands up and down Alex's back. "We can wait to see my parents. They'll understand."

"Thanks, Bryn. I'm really sorry. I want to meet them, too. They must be very special raising a daughter like you."

That statement earned her a big kiss. The blonde then sat down on Alex's lap—her favorite place to be. "They're not going anywhere and maybe you'll feel different once you start therapy. When's your first appointment?"

"Friday—after work." Alex stroked Bryn's long, golden hair, then gently turned her face so she could look directly into her eyes. "I still have a lot bottled up inside of me...last night, when I broke down, was the first time I've really cried since I was a child." She paused. "What I'm trying to say is, I may not be very easy to live with for a while, so I'll understand if you spend more time at your place."

Tears filled green eyes. "I'm not leaving you to deal with this by yourself—understand?"

Alex sighed in relief and flashed the barest hint of a smile. *She really does love me.* "I understand."

"Good. C'mon. Let's clean up the dishes and go for a walk. Then we can snuggle in bed with some popcorn, hot chocolate, and old movies." She tugged on the surgeon's arm, pulling her out of the chair.

"That sounds great...but no more snake movies."

Bryn giggled. "Okay, no more snake movies."

Chapter 14

"Are you comfortable, Squeak?" Bryn was wrapped in Alex's strong arms as they watched television together.

"Mhm. I couldn't be more comfortable." The nurse nuzzled her companion's neck affectionately. Alex responded with a quick kiss to the blonde's head.

Alex hesitated. "Bryn...can I ask you something?"

"Anything."

"Well, it's pretty obvious how much you love children. I was wondering...are you planning on becoming a mother...someday?"

Bryn was a little surprised at the question. "Of course I've thought about it...many times, in fact. There's no reason physically for me to avoid getting pregnant. But I would never consider doing it alone, unless I adopted an older child. Why do you ask, honey?" Bryn made a point to use that term of endearment when she knew Alex was feeling especially vulnerable.

"Because I've watched you, and you're just so wonderful with kids...and I..." Alex paused. "I don't think I could ever be a mother, Bryn. I'm afraid I'd screw things up."

Bryn's heart went out to her brooding companion. "That's simply not true. I've watched you with your patients, too. I've never seen anyone more warm and loving...in spite of having Olivia as a mother."

"But what if you want kids some day and I don't?" Alex thought her heart was going to pound out of her chest.

"Lex. Listen to me." Bryn straddled her companion so she could face her. She then smoothed her thumbs across the dark brows. "You're what I want...what I need...above anything else."

Big tears spilled from Alex's deep blue eyes before she could stop them. She angrily wiped them away, but more replaced them.

Bryn felt a pang deep in her heart. "Honey, please don't be angry or embarrassed for crying in front of me. It's really okay." She tenderly wiped the tears away.

Alex slowly regained her composure. "I can't help it...it's really hard for me. I'm just not used to bursting into tears like this. It's...very embarrassing for me. I don't know why, but I can't seem to control my emotions when I'm with you."

"Good...I don't want you to. Save it for the rest of the world...okay?"

"Okay." The surgeon smiled. "You're impossible

to say no to anyway." Alex felt like she had crossed another hurdle and that made her hopeful about their relationship. She never wanted to keep Bryn from realizing her dreams, but it seemed as though all of Bryn's dreams centered on Alex. She felt another piece of her heart fall back into place.

****

When her shift ended on Friday, Bryn hurried to run errands during her two hours of free time before she had to go back to the hospital to pick up Alex. As she arrived at the surgeon's home, she was dismayed to find several boxes on the front porch from a Falmouth, Massachusetts address.

"Damn," Bryn cursed under her breath. "She doesn't need this now."

The blonde moved the boxes to the basement, then quickly showered and changed into jeans, hiking boots, and a gray Old Navy sweatshirt. When she was done, she went back downstairs to the basement. Kneeling next to the boxes that held bits and pieces of her soul mate's past, she tenderly ran her fingers across the top of one of them. She loved Lex so completely, that she wanted to understand everything that made her complex partner the person she was. Alex had obviously grown up with precious little love since her father died. Yet she was able to give it abundantly to Bryn. The enigmatic surgeon had managed to wrap the petite nurse around her little finger. Of course, the reverse was true as well.

Bryn checked her watch and then decided to throw a load of laundry into the washing machine before heading back to the hospital.

She arrived at the hospital at five o'clock sharp. Alex greeted her warmly, attempting to hide her anxiety. Trying to fool Bryn was useless; the young nurse already knew her lover better than that.

"I know how much you're dreading this, love." Bryn took the surgeon's slender hand and held it. "I appreciate you doing this for us...I'm sure it can't be easy."

"I can handle it...I'm an adult now, and I'll just have to get through it. But it feels really good having you along." She kissed the blonde's cheek tenderly.

They arrived at Dr. Kaplan's office just as Bryn was returning the kiss. She gently let go of Alex's hand and parked the car. They got out and walked in together, hand in hand.

Bonnie Kaplan was a tall, attractive woman in her fifties with graying, curly hair and light blue eyes. She had a Ph.D. in psychology, and specialized in family therapy. She introduced herself, greeting Alex and Bryn warmly. The psychologist's warm manner immediately put Bryn at ease. Alex, who appeared composed outwardly, was trembling inside. Her empathetic partner affectionately reached for her hand, squeezing it tight. Alex acknowledged the gesture with a sad smile.

"I understand that you want Bryn present for the session. Is that right, Alex?" Bonnie had suggested being on a first name basis when Dr. Morgan had scheduled the first appointment.

"Yes. I want her here with me. Until..."

"Go ahead," Bonnie encouraged.

Alex looked at Bryn, her blue eyes pleading for

forgiveness. "There's something that I...just don't feel comfortable sharing." Alex looked down at her lap, clearly uncomfortable.

"It's okay, Lex. I understand." Bryn rubbed her thumb over the top of Alex's hand.

"I...Will you leave if I ask you to?"

"Yes, honey." *God, why does this hurt so? I'm being a big baby about this.*

"I'm sorry, Bryn. I just don't want you to hear about the first time..." Alex's heart pounded wildly. Her beautiful face revealed intense emotional pain. "About the time...I failed sexually." Alex glanced over at the door to Bonnie's private restroom. She wanted to take note of its exact location in case she had to throw up.

Bryn felt like she had just been punched in the gut. She slowly closed her eyes, biting her lip. Taking a deep breath, she opened them and gazed directly into haunted blue eyes.

"You just say the word, and I'll leave."

"Thank you," Alex whispered gratefully, her grip on Bryn's hand tightening. "I'm...sorry."

"S'okay, honey. I understand."

Bonnie gently interceded then, questioning the couple about how long they had been together, what hobbies they enjoyed, and about their jobs. Once Alex and Bryn relaxed a little, she quickly moved on to the root of the problem. Predictably, the therapy reached a point where Alex was no longer comfortable with her partner's presence. Trembling, she turned to Bryn.

"It's time," she whispered hoarsely.

"Okay." Bryn's voice quavered a little. "I'll be

right outside if you need me for *anything.*"

Alex impulsively gathered Bryn into a fierce hug. "I love you, Squeak," she whispered in her ear.

"I love you, too, Lex." The small blonde left as quickly as possible, just making it to the restroom outside before breaking down. Bryn locked herself in a stall and tried to stifle her deep sobs. She truly understood why her partner didn't want her present, but she couldn't bear to leave her at such a crucial and painful moment in her life. Bryn's heart was *breaking* for her lover.

Eventually, the sobs subsided to hiccups, and Bryn wiped her eyes. She left the stall and carefully washed her face, anxious to remove the evidence of her tears. *That's the last thing Lex needs today,* she thought. Alex *hated* to see her partner cry.

After pulling herself together, Bryn went out to the waiting room and snagged a magazine from the table. She tried to read but was unable to focus on anything but the woman she loved. Her head ached from the tension.

Eventually, to Bryn's great relief, her pale companion opened the door and motioned for her to come in. "I'm going to the car," she told Bryn flatly. "Dr. Kaplan wants to talk to you."

"Uh oh," the blonde said under her breath, as she entered the room. *I wonder what happened to "Bonnie"? Lex has her walls back up again.*

"Sit down, Bryn. I won't keep you long."

The young nurse wiped sweaty palms on her jeans. "Is Lex okay?"

The psychologist got directly to the point. "I suspect that Alex has experienced some very deep childhood trauma. That's why she can't remember you. As for her intimacy problems—that's the result of a terribly controlling, remote parent...although the trauma could definitely be a factor as well." The older woman paused. "Plus, she has some considerable guilt over her abortion. If we can help her remember the trauma and counsel her afterwards, I think she'll be all right. Alex is a remarkable human being."

Bryn swallowed audibly, only hearing one sentence. "Oh, God. You don't think her mother..."

"I really don't know, Bryn. The family was under an incredible amount of stress after Dr. Morgan's untimely death. But I do know this—she's going to need your love and support more than ever."

"She's got it...I love her with all my heart. I'll help her get through this."

Bonnie Kaplan smiled. "I believe it. With so much love between you two, you definitely will."

****

Friday evening did not go well. Alex had been unusually quiet and only picked at her dinner. Bryn felt tired, achy, and fretful about her soul mate. Eventually the two fell into bed together, each just needing to be held. Neither slept well...Alex's cries during her nightmares awakened Bryn twice.

The next morning started as badly as the previous evening had ended. Rain beat incessantly against the windows, and Bryn awakened with a nasty cold, a low-grade fever, and a headache. The instant Alex opened her eyes her pager went off—she was needed at the hospital to see a new patient who was being transferred from a rural area. Naturally, she hated leaving the warmth and comfort of Bryn and her bed. Not to mention the fact that she preferred to stay home with her sick partner. Alex showered and dressed quickly. Then she made a cup of tea for her love, plumped up her pillows, and gave her a dose of acetaminophen.

"I hate to leave you, Squeak," she said softly. "The minute I'm done, I'll head home." She brought some reading materials to Bryn's bedside and handed her the TV remote control. "Will you be okay?"

"It's only a bad cold, honey. I'll be fine. I just feel really crummy...ugh," the petite blonde replied hoarsely.

The surgeon gave her a huge hug and kiss. "Page me if you need anything. I love you."

"I love you, too. But I don't think you should be kissing me."

"I don't care. I'm not abstaining from kissing you for a whole week, so just forget about it. I'll be back soon...I hope." She touched two fingers to her lips and moved them towards Bryn as she left. Worrying about her beloved had completely taken her mind off the appointment with Dr. Kaplan. Her heart wrenched at having to leave Bryn alone when she was sick.

While Alex was gone, Bryn took a hot bath and changed into one of her lover's white oxford shirts. Although oversized, the shirt looked charming on her. She brushed out her long, golden hair, and then climbed back into bed. The bath had relaxed her, and Bryn soon fell asleep. She was still sleeping when the surgeon returned around noon.

Alex walked quietly over to the bed and gently touched the blonde's forehead. "Still running a temperature," she whispered, placing a tender kiss to the flushed cheek. She turned around to change clothes, but was stopped by a small hand.

"You're back," Bryn said hoarsely. "Is it still raining out?"

"Yes...it's pouring." Alex sat down on the edge of the bed and took Bryn into her arms. "How are you feeling?"

"Like hell. I took a bath, and I've been sleeping almost the whole time you were gone." Bryn rested her head on the surgeon's broad shoulder for several moments.

"Oh...I almost forgot...I brought you a care package. It's in the kitchen." Alex quickly left the room but was back in a flash with a large grocery bag.

Bryn smiled. "What's in it?"

Alex gave Bryn her biggest, lopsided grin. "Check it out." She placed the bag on the bed. Bryn peeked inside and started to laugh. Inside was cough medicine, a huge box of tissues, cold tablets, ibuprofen, a jar of mentholatum, a tube of ointment for sore noses, cans of chicken noodle soup, a box of saltines, a package of Pinwheels, and a tiny stuffed rabbit.

"Ooo," Bryn exclaimed, delighted. "You remembered that I collect rabbits. This one is so cute and soft." She cuddled it to her chest. "And all this other stuff, too. You're so thoughtful, Lex. I love you." She squeezed her lover as tightly as possible.

Alex flushed with pleasure. "You like it?"

"It's the best. I'm feeling better already." Bryn gave Alex one more squeeze. "Now change out of those clothes into something more comfortable and get back into bed with me. I'm sick, it's pouring down rain outside, and all I want is to spend the whole day snuggling with my favorite person."

"You've got yourself a deal. But first, I need to get some fluids into you. What would you like?"

Bryn groaned good-naturally. "Some Peach Snapple would be great."

"One Peach Snapple coming up, Squeak."

As Alex left the room, Bryn thought how nurturing she was. *She'll make a wonderful mother some day...in spite of Olivia.* The blonde sighed deeply. *I just wish Alex could see the person I see.*

Chapter 15

Bryn was getting comfortable again when she heard the sound of glass shattering. She jumped out of bed and went towards the kitchen. "Lex. What happened?" She peeked in the kitchen, finding it empty.

"It's nothing...just stay put," a shaky voice replied from downstairs.

"Uh oh. The boxes." Bryn hurried to the basement.

"Don't come down here," Alex warned. The warning was ignored; Bryn ran down the stairs.

"Oh my God," Bryn exclaimed. "You're bleeding."

The surgeon stood next to the refrigerator, holding a portion of a broken bottle. Blood dripped steadily from her right hand onto the floor, mixing with the shattered glass and orange liquid. Alex's face was very pale, and her expression pained. "It's only a superficial cut. Go on back upstairs while I clean up...you're not wearing any shoes."

"Then I'll get some...I'm not leaving you to deal with this alone." The blonde hurried upstairs to put on some slippers. She also grabbed a thick towel from the linen closet. When she returned downstairs to her injured companion, she was surprised to find that Alex had not moved...she just stood there, blood dripping from her hand.

"Lex...let me wrap your hand in this towel," Bryn coaxed gently. "And you need to let go of the broken bottle."

"What? Oh...sorry." Alex put down the broken glass and let Bryn wrap her hand in the towel. Bryn then led Alex to an upstairs bathroom where she held the injured hand under cold, running water, trying to gauge how serious the gash was. Once the blood was rinsed away, she saw that the wound was fairly deep.

"Looks like you'll need a couple of stitches, honey. What do you think?"

Alex sighed. "Yeah...a couple should do it. I'll just take care of it myself."

"I don't know...this IS your right hand...and your livelihood. Maybe you should see a specialist."

"No...it's just a flesh wound. I can certainly take care of it. I'll get the needle and sutures."

While Alex went to get her supplies, Bryn washed out the sink, kicking herself that she didn't tell Lex about the boxes when they had been delivered. Alex must have gotten so upset upon seeing them that she squeezed the bottle of juice in her hand until it had simply shattered.

Bryn was pulled out of her reverie by Alex's

return. "I'm going to need a little help...I'm not used to using my left hand," the surgeon stated matter-of-factly.

"I'm ready...just tell me what you need."

The surgeon had Bryn pour betadine over the wound, then quickly and efficiently put in several stitches with minimal assistance. They were beautifully done, in spite of Alex's handicap of having to use her left hand. When she was finished, Bryn carefully applied a bandage.

"Thanks, Squeak...you're a wonderful nurse." She took a deep breath. "I'm going to try once more to bring you your Snapple. Then you can rest while I change and clean up the mess downstairs. I've got to get my clothes and this towel in the wash before the blood stains set in." Alex looked tired and depressed.

"Things will go faster if I help...I may be sick, but I'm not bedridden. Besides, one of your hands is bandaged. C'mon, honey." Bryn gave Alex a big hug.

The surgeon knew Bryn well enough not to argue with her. In record time, the basement was cleaned, laundry was started, and Alex was wearing fresh clothes. Bryn got back into bed while Alex brought in a tray with a glass of ice, a straw, and two bottles of Snapple. She didn't want her love to get dehydrated.

The blonde accepted the tray, and then gently caressed the surgeon's cheek. "Get into bed with me, Lex...we need to talk."

"I...need to be alone for a while. Maybe later." Alex's jaw twitched and her blue eyes were glazed.

"Are you upset with me?"

Alex sighed. The sight of those watery green eyes pulled at her heartstrings. "No...I know you were only trying to protect me. It was just a shock, seeing those boxes. I feel pretty stupid losing control like that. It seems as if that's all I do lately."

"It's perfectly understandable," the blonde whispered hoarsely. "You have a right to be upset with me. I just didn't want you dealing with the appointment and the boxes all in the same day." Bryn stifled a sob. "I hate seeing you go through so much pain. It tears me apart."

Alex's beautiful blue eyes softened. She sat down on the bed and took Bryn into her arms. "I love you so much." She kissed the soft, blond hair. "I'm not mad at you, Squeak. No one's ever cared about me the way you do. I'm afraid I just don't know how to handle it."

Bryn sniffled. "I understand, but please believe me, I'm here to stay. I'll never leave you."

Alex felt her heart skip a beat. She grabbed a few tissues and held them to the blonde's nose. "Here...now blow." Bryn complied. "That's better. No more crying...okay? It'll just make your nose stuffier."

Bryn sighed in relief. "It's a deal, but only if you agree to come and snuggle with me. We're both tired, and you've just done minor surgery on your own hand—without a painkiller."

"You talked me into it. Let me get into some boxers first." Alex removed her jeans and added a pair of soft gray boxers to her gray tee shirt. Bryn tried not to be too obvious as she watched her companion undress, but she just couldn't help it. The dark haired surgeon had an incredibly beautiful body.

Alex smirked as she climbed into bed. "You are

too much, Bryn O'Neill."

"What?"

"I saw you looking at my legs." She tapped the blonde on the nose.

Bryn smiled sheepishly. "It's impossible not to look...I mean, you have gorgeous legs...they're so long, and well...so sexy."

"I'm glad you like them." Alex paused. "You've done it again you know." The surgeon looked intently into Bryn's eyes and played with her hair. The blonde responded by wrapping a raven lock around her own fingers.

"What have I done this time?" Bryn teased.

"Made me smile...when I didn't think I could. Made me happy...in spite of everything. You're so very special to me." Alex kissed Bryn's forehead tenderly.

"I love you, Lex." She caressed the surgeon's cheek reverently. "I always will." Their lips met in a gentle kiss before they fell asleep in each other's arms.

The rest of the weekend was spent recuperating. Alex waited on Bryn hand and foot, in spite of her injury. The two women enjoyed their time together and made the most of it. By Monday Bryn was feeling better, although she still tired easily. Alex's hand had begun to heal as well. Fortunately, the cut had not affected her ability to perform surgery.

After work on Monday, Bryn, knowing that her lover would not arrive home until she completed her late afternoon rounds, went to Alex's to take a nap.

After her nap, she went downstairs to replenish the upstairs refrigerator with their favorite beverages.

Bryn couldn't help but pass by the boxes of mementos from Olivia. Surprisingly, one of the boxes had been opened and the blonde glanced inside—then sat down. "Oh, Lex," she whispered. In a polished oak frame, was a family photograph of Alex with her brother, mother, and father. The children and their parents looked very happy. Bryn noted that Olivia was an extremely attractive woman, nothing like the monster she had imagined. Alex and David clearly resembled their father. Olivia had wavy, ash-brown hair and hazel eyes.

Feeling like an intruder, Bryn put the photo back in the box. *I wonder when Lex was down here looking at this stuff?* She picked up the cartons of Snapple and Coors Lite, and went back upstairs.

As she stocked the refrigerator, she started to worry. She just couldn't bear to think of Lex sitting in the basement going through her things alone. What if she suddenly remembered the childhood trauma that Bonnie had mentioned? Bryn shuddered. She wanted to be there for Lex when she needed her.

Since Alex's first appointment with Dr. Kaplan, the blonde felt certain that old wounds had been re-opened. Each night, Bryn would soothe her lover through at least one nightmare—a nightmare that Alex was never able to remember. Still, in spite of their problems, their relationship continued to grow stronger.

Bryn was certainly no stranger to adversity. Her illness and surgery had only strengthened the iron will she was born with. Her parents had given her the moniker of "Little Lioness"—due to her thick golden hair, her Leo birthday—August 2nd, and her very strong personality. The problems she and Alex faced were simply another challenge for Bryn. She welcomed them as an opportunity to make a difference in the life of the most important person in the world. Her deep love for Alex knew no limits.

At that moment, the object of her affections peeked into the kitchen. A huge smile lit up her beautiful blue eyes when she looked at Bryn. "Come here, you. God, I missed you today." The surgeon lifted the petite blonde off the floor easily.

"I missed you too, honey." She enveloped the gorgeous woman in a huge bear hug.

"Bryn..." Alex kissed a soft ear. "I need to feel..." The surgeon seemed so vulnerable; her eyes exposing the insecurity Bryn knew Alex struggled with daily.

"What do you need, honey?" Bryn nibbled her way across her lover's warm neck. "Just tell me, and I'll give it to you."

Alex's breath quickened. *Oh, how she wanted Bryn to do just that—to "give it to her."* Alex's body longed for that precious gift from Bryn...but she knew she wasn't ready. She couldn't bear the disappointment in Bryn's eyes if she failed. Alex was embarrassed to ask, but it was the only way—for now at least. She took a deep breath. "Will you hold me while I..."

"Yes," the blonde replied in a smoky voice. "Right here?"

"Right here...right now," the surgeon growled.

"Ooo, Lex." *What's gotten into you? Whatever it*

is, I love it. She kissed Alex's soft lips, gently slipping her tongue into her mouth.

"Mmm," Alex moaned deeply. Bryn unbuttoned the surgeon's blouse and slipped it off her broad shoulders, then unhooked her bra.

Bryn looked down, seeing that Alex's hand had disappeared beneath the waistband of her own slacks. *Oh God*, she thought, as her knees grew weak. "Lex, my love, tell me how I can help?"

"Uhhh...just hold me...kiss me...right here." She moved Bryn's hand to her breast. "Ohhh." The surgeon felt like she was on fire as her hips rocked steadily against her own hand.

Bryn embraced Alex, kissing her deeply. The blonde dropped her head to her lover's left breast capturing it in her mouth and suckling her erect nipple.

"Oh, God...Bryn...I can't take much more...feels so good."

"You like that, baby?"

"Oh yes," she whimpered.

Bryn whispered something erotic in Alex's ear, and her eyes flew open.

"Oh, God. Oh, Bryn. Oh...Oh." The surgeon's hips jerked spasmodically as she found her release.

Bryn held her and kissed her as the intense waves of pleasure slowly died down. "I love you, Lex."

Alex struggled to catch her breath. "Right back at ya." She laughed as she suddenly remembered what the blonde had said to her. "Bryn. Underneath that sweet, angelic exterior is a little fireball."

"Heh...you certainly seemed to like it though."

"Oh, I did. It was so intense...more than ever before."

"Speaking of fireballs, what got into you? Not that I'm complaining...I loved it."

Alex blushed. "I get like this sometimes...especially on days after seeing so much pain and suffering at the hospital. Plus, I just needed to feel close to you." She kissed her lover tenderly.

"How would you like to feel even closer?" Bryn teased.

"I'd like that very much," Alex breathed into her ear. "Right here? Right now?"

Bryn nibbled a tender ear. "Right here...right now."

Alex lifted the petite blonde up and she wrapped her legs around the surgeon's waist. She nipped at Bryn's soft neck and kissed her way to even softer lips.

"Oh, Bryn ..." she whispered into her ear. "You make me so hot."

"Lex," Bryn moaned. "I need you...now."

Their lovemaking became frenzied. Alex frantically undressed Bryn, and then pushed her against the kitchen counter. She slid her hand down the blonde's flat belly, then slipped a finger inside.

"More...please?" Bryn ran her fingers through glossy, black hair.

Alex added another finger, then two. "How's that?"

"Oh...so good..." Bryn struggled not to touch Alex...she wanted to so much.

The surgeon suckled a beautiful breast as her hand brought Bryn to the brink of orgasm. Bryn could barely stand...what she was feeling was incredible. Alex wound her up tighter and tighter, until she exploded. "Ohhh...Ohhh...Ohhh," she moaned deeply.

Alex supported her as the spasms subsided. She kissed her gently on the forehead, smoothing her damp bangs away. "Did you like that?" the surgeon whispered shyly.

"That was...that was...I can't even describe it."

Alex flushed with pleasure. In spite of her own problems with intimacy, she had none at all when it came to meeting the needs of her partner. She proved to be a tender, passionate lover. The two snuggled for a few minutes before Alex finally spoke. "Well, now that we've gotten 'that' out of our systems, we can concentrate on dinner."

"Great. I am kind of hungry after all that exercise...a little tired, too." The blonde stifled a yawn.

"Why don't you lie down on the couch, Squeak? I'll do chores, then go pick up some Chinese food for dinner."

"Everything's done—but Chinese food sounds great. And I've already taken a nap."

"Okay...I'll go change into something more comfortable, then go pick up our favorite dishes." After washing up and changing clothes, Alex gave Bryn a quick kiss before heading out the door.

While Alex was gone, Bryn took time to freshen up. Afterwards, she grabbed a Snapple from the refrigerator and went out to the porch. Although they continued to maintain separate residences, in reality the two women were living together. Alex had gone out of her way to make Bryn feel at home, and the young nurse was surprised at how comfortable she felt in the surgeon's home.

On several occasions, they had tried sleeping apart. Bryn would get into bed, waiting to see who caved in first. Usually, it was Alex. She was so cute about it, the blonde thought. Predictably, at eleven o'clock, the phone would ring. Bryn would answer immediately.

"Hello..."

"I can't sleep...may I come over?" the surgeon would ask tentatively.

Alex could hear the joy in Bryn's voice. "There's a spot next to me with your name on it. Drive carefully...I love you."

"Right back at ya. I'll be there in a few minutes."

Bryn sighed as she felt her heart swell with emotion...never had she been so happy or felt so complete. She had been unaware of what real love could be until incredible fortune brought Alex back into her life.

"Bryn?" The surgeon shook her gently. "Dinner's here...are you all right?"

"I'm fine...I was just thinking." The young nurse impulsively hugged her lover.

"About what?" Alex set out plates, napkins, and chopsticks on the coffee table.

"You."

"Good answer," the surgeon teased sitting down next to Bryn. When they had finished eating, Alex took Bryn's hands in her own. "I need to talk to you about something very important, Squeak." The beautiful woman swallowed nervously.

"Okay." Bryn's heart pounded with anticipation.

Alex bit her lip and paused for a moment. "We've

only been together for a short period of time, but in that time, a lot has happened between us. And I think you know just how much I care about you." Bryn detected a slight tremor in her lover's hands.

"Yes." Bryn's voice was barely above a whisper.

"You've not only told me how much you love me, but more importantly, you've shown me in so many ways. You've taken care of me when I was sick, held me when I've cried, supported me through a devastating problem..." Alex caressed Bryn's soft, golden hair. "And now..." The surgeon looked down, taking a deep breath. "Now you've given me the courage to face my demons...and I truly believe I can...because I have you to hold my hand." Alex's blue eyes glittered with unshed tears.

Bryn could only listen, afraid to speak...afraid to break the spell between them.

Alex kissed the blonde's knuckles—one by one. "What I'm trying to say is—I love you, I want to commit to you, and I want you to live with me. I know we can't get married, but that doesn't change how I feel about you. I never want to be apart from you, Bryn. Because you're a part of my soul." Tears spilled down Alex's cheeks.

Bryn burst into happy tears herself. "Oh, Lex...I accept." She squeezed the surgeon tight. "That's the most beautiful thing anyone's ever said to me."

"You accept?" Alex half laughed, half cried.

"Yes." Bryn sniffled.

"Okay...then I have a big surprise for you," she said shakily. "But first, I think we both need a tissue."

After their tears were dried, Alex pulled a photograph from the drawer of an end table, and handed it to Bryn. The blonde's green eyes grew wide. "What a beautiful cottage...and it's on the beach, too. But who does it belong to?"

"Us," Alex, unable to stop her happy tears, replied.

"Us? What do you mean?"

"My dad's cottage...I bought it anonymously...for us. It can be our vacation home...we can fill it with happy memories again...I know we can."

Bryn was overwhelmed. "It's incredible...I always wanted a house on the beach. I'm so proud of you for doing that, Lex...you're turning a painful experience into something positive." She kissed the surgeon's hand.

"Because of you, Bryn." After long moments of hugging and crying, they pulled apart. Alex tenderly wiped Bryn's tears away and looked into her eyes. "Just remember, I haven't forgotten about a ring—I'll buy you anything you want."

"That can wait...you buying this cottage for us means the world to me."

"Then why don't we celebrate? I'll be right back." Alex returned shortly with a plate of Pinwheels.

Bryn laughed. "You can be so cute sometimes...my Lex."

They spent the rest of the evening feeding each other cookies and laughing late into the night. And another piece of Alex's heart fell back into place.

Chapter 16

The next few weeks were a busy time for the two women. Alex helped Bryn move her things into the surgeon's white, Victorian home. Fortunately, they shared similar tastes and after making a few changes, it soon became Alex and Bryn's home. Bryn rented her house to her sister, Cam, and Cam's fiancé Ben.

Eager to resolve her problems, Alex began to see Dr. Bonnie Kaplan twice a week. She desperately wanted what other couples took for granted—a normal intimate relationship with her lover. In spite of Alex's best efforts to recover quickly, the therapy sessions were difficult and her nightmares intensified. Too often, Bryn would awaken in the middle of the night to find her soul mate absent from their bed. Each time, Bryn found the surgeon in the basement pouring over the contents of the boxes of childhood mementos.

One rainy night in October, Bryn found Alex sitting on the basement floor at two o'clock in the morning. She was clutching a tan, Steiff teddy bear and a photograph of her brother, David. Bryn sank to her knees and embraced her lover. "Want to talk about it, honey?"

"No." Alex was trying hard not to cry. She shuddered as she gripped the bear even tighter.

Bryn lifted Alex's chin and looked into her eyes: "I'm your partner now...we've come a long way together. Please lean on me—that's what I'm here for."

Alex's blue eyes searched Bryn's for a long moment, her dark brows furrowed in pain. Bryn opened her arms wide. "Let me help you, Lex...please?"

Breaking down completely, Alex fell sobbing into Bryn's arms. Bryn held her tightly and whispered soothing words of comfort until, finally exhausted, her lover fell asleep.

After that night, Alex felt more comfortable letting Bryn see her at her most vulnerable. No one else was ever allowed to witness this side of her. The stoic surgeon would confide in Dr. Kaplan, but no matter how upset she became during her therapy, she would always hold back her tears until she was alone in the safe haven of Bryn's arms. She even told her partner just how unloved Olivia had made her feel. Bryn cried bitter tears after one particular revelation.

"Please, Mommy, wake up." The little figure gently shook her sleeping parent.

"Alexandra? What on earth do you want? It's one o'clock in the morning." She didn't even bother to notice that the child was unusually pale.

"My head...it hurts really bad...and my tummy hurts, too. I feel like I'm gonna throw up." The seven-year-old's lip poked out as she clutched her stomach.

"Go wake up Anna. She'll take care of you. And if you're going to be sick, please go to the bathroom."

The little girl stood at her mother's bed and cried. Soon, a heavy-set woman appeared. She knew that if Lexi was crying, then she must have a very good reason. "Come here, darling," she whispered. "What's the matter?" she asked as she lifted the little girl into her arms.

"Anna, I'm sick...and I want my daddy." She laid her dark head against the broad shoulder, sobbing.

"I'll take care of you. Let's go to my room, sweetheart."

As Anna walked down the hall with Lexi in her arms, they heard Olivia call out, "Thank you, Anna. She probably just picked up a 24 hour bug or something." The little girl's mother went back to sleep immediately.

Alex never forgot that terrible experience—her first migraine headache, and Olivia wouldn't even get out of bed to be with her. Bryn was distressed to learn that young Lexi went through so much pain without her mother's comforting love. Alex assured Bryn that Anna stayed with her all night and even into the next day, until the headache was gone.

Bryn began to hate Olivia Morgan. It was an

intense hatred, one she had never felt toward another living soul. *It's a miracle Alex can even love at all,* Bryn thought, feeling a fierce determination to protect her lover from future hurt of any kind.

Talking to Bryn was very therapeutic for the surgeon. Her partner was a wonderful listener and never judgmental. Bryn reassured her...telling her how much she was loved, and what a fine person she was. Alex couldn't help but feel that if someone as spectacular as Bryn loved her, then she must be pretty special herself.

One Sunday morning Bryn surprised Alex by requesting personal riding lessons. The surgeon was delighted that there was some way she could repay Bryn for all her love and support. Bryn overcame her initial unease around Apollo and proved to be a natural. The two women spent as much time as possible riding together—Bryn on Starlight, a beautiful, strawberry roan mare from the stables.

Finding time between therapy sessions, work, horseback riding, and fixing up their home, Alex took Bryn to an Atlanta Braves baseball game. The wonderful evening had been perfect—seats behind the Braves dugout, crisp, early autumn weather, hot dogs, and Bryn's favorite—cotton candy.

"I can't believe you're actually wearing a Boston Red Sox cap and jersey to a Braves play-off game." The blonde eyed her partner critically. *"Although, you do look incredibly cute...especially with that pony-tail."* Bryn tugged playfully at the shiny, black hair.

Alex's face beamed with a lop-sided grin—the one

that always made Bryn's heart skip a beat. "Well, you're the only Braves fan in our family, Squeak. Besides, I did manage to get these fabulous seats for us...and I bought you blue cotton candy, too."

Bryn laughed. "That's true. Did I tell you how much I love you for it?"

"Yes...but I wouldn't mind hearing it again." Alex took a big bite of her hot dog.

"I love you. And, oh, by the way, you have mustard on your nose, Dr. Morgan."

"What?" Alex grabbed a napkin and swiped at her nose frantically. "Is it gone now?"

Alex looked so distressed. She had fallen for Bryn's prank hook, line, and sinker. The petite blonde snorted with laughter as Coke spewed out her nose.

"Nice trick, Bryn...serves you right. There wasn't any mustard on my nose, was there?" Alex asked indignantly.

"No." Bryn coughed and spluttered, wiping her face. Then she burst into hysterical giggles. Soon, Alex was laughing with her. Impulsively, the surgeon grabbed a handful of cotton candy and rubbed it all over Bryn's face. "Blue looks good on you, Squeak."

"I'll get you for that, Lex." Bryn returned the favor, knowing how much her immaculate partner hated to be sticky. They both laughed and carried on like two little children, to the amusement of the other fans around them.

On their way home, Bryn gave Alex a tender kiss and a hug. "Thanks for tonight, Lex. I had the time of my life."

"You're welcome, my love. So did I." She reached for the blonde's hand and held it. Alex *couldn't remember a time when she felt so at peace or so happy.*

The following day, the couple purchased two round trip airplane tickets to Boston, Massachusetts. They wanted to spend Thanksgiving at their Cape Cod cottage, walking hand in hand together on the beach. Alex felt a great deal of trepidation at the thought of seeing her childhood home again, but Dr. Kaplan assured her this was a difficult but necessary step towards full recovery.

By early November, Alex and Bryn were happily settled into their new life together. But total bliss eluded them. Alex was still unable to allow Bryn to touch her in the most intimate of ways. To compensate, the two were extremely creative and often, they almost forgot something was missing.

Bryn's parents still had not seen Alex since she was a little girl. Bryn explained what her partner was going through, and that it would take some time. She was reminded, once again, how fortunate she was to have the total support of her mother and father. Their patience in this matter never ceased to amaze her. Being kind and open-minded, Kevin and Kathleen O'Neill continued their acceptance of Bryn and Alex's relationship. Having their child nearly die when she was four years old helped her parents keep a perspective on what was truly important in life. Their beautiful daughter was healthy and blissfully happy. Nothing else mattered to them.

Alex's inability to come to terms with her past also delayed the commitment ceremony that she and Bryn desired. Although they had privately committed their hearts and souls to one another, they wanted all of Bryn's family and their friends to witness their public professions of love for one another. But the couple had to wait until Alex felt comfortable seeing Bryn's parents again.

The surgeon had no qualms about meeting Bryn's younger sister, Cam, born a year after Bryn's surgery, and her fiancé Ben. The two couples got along well. Alex grew particularly fond of Cam, in part because she reminded her of Bryn—except Cam was more reserved and had auburn hair instead of blonde.

On the Friday before Thanksgiving, Bryn drove Alex to her therapy session. Dr. Kaplan was particularly pleased with the progress being made. Alex felt the process should be going faster, but kept her frustration to herself.

After the appointment was over, the couple went to their favorite Mexican restaurant for dinner. As they ate chips and salsa they were reminded of the first time they shared that particular treat. That night had been a turning point in their lives. "Remember the first time we shared chips and salsa?" Alex winked shyly at Bryn.

The petite blonde blushed slightly. "Ooo, how could I forget? I think they're some sort of aphrodisiac for us...I'm feeling..." she whispered in the surgeon's ear.

"Bryn O'Neill. Your innocent look is such a disguise."

"You love it though...admit it."

"Okay, I admit it...I love it." As usual, Bryn had made Alex smile when the surgeon was feeling a little down.

After dinner, the couple returned to their home and decided to have coffee together out on the screened in porch. The main topic of conversation was the upcoming trip to Boston. Bryn moved closer to her partner. Sipping from her cup, she turned to face Alex. "There's been something I've been meaning to ask you."

The surgeon grinned crookedly. "And what might that be, my love?"

"You were born in Boston, right?"

"Yeah...on July 4th, 1968 to be precise."

"Okay...then why don't you speak with an accent?" The blonde played with a lock of her lover's hair.

"Well, that's an easy question. Both my parents are from California."

"Oh...I never knew that. I just assumed you were all from Massachusetts."

"No. Believe it or not, Olivia has a degree in nursing. That's how she met Dad. They moved to Boston from the San Francisco Bay area after he finished his residency at Stanford University."

"From what you've told me, they seem like two very different individuals. Medicine must have been what they had in common."

Alex sighed. "Yes, they were completely different. Why did he marry her? It must have been something more than just an interest in medicine. If I knew, maybe I could deal with things better. My only perspective is that of a child."

Bryn stroked Alex's cheek. "You're dealing with things just fine," she encouraged.

"Thanks to you...my Bryn." She tapped the blonde's nose. "You've always believed in me...accepted me the way I am. You'll never know what that means to me."

"All I ever want to do is make you happy...you're so special to me...my Lex."

Alex leaned in for a tender kiss. She had never thought it possible to love anyone as much as she loved Bryn. Her heart felt like it was going to burst with emotion. When the kiss ended, she looked at Bryn expectantly, her blue eyes wide.

"Is something wrong?" the blonde asked, concerned.

"Um...what do you think about getting a couple of dogs? After the holidays, I mean."

Bryn laughed heartily. "I think that's a fabulous idea. What made you think of that?"

Alex shrugged. "I don't know. I've always wanted a dog, but Olivia wouldn't allow it when I was growing up. She thought they were unsanitary." The blue eyes clouded over with pain for a moment, then brightened. "Since we're a family now, I just thought we should have a couple of dogs living with us."

Bryn was delighted. "You never cease to amaze me. You are such a big softie. And I love it." She squeezed the surgeon as tightly as she could.

"Oof...easy there," Alex chuckled. "I'm still full from dinner."

"Sorry...you're just so lovable. Besides, I'm really excited—I've missed having a dog around. I've had them almost my whole life."

Alex gazed into Bryn's soulful green eyes and kissed her. The kiss quickly deepened and intensified until the petite blonde climbed onto her soul mate's lap. Alex cradled Bryn in her arms and carried her to their bed. Some time later, they lay in each other's embrace, completely sated.

"That was incredible...you are magnificent." Bryn tucked a lock of hair behind the surgeon's ear.

Alex grinned shyly. "I'm glad you enjoyed it. Thanks for being so patient. I know how much you want to make love to me...it must be an almost impossible situation."

"Not as impossible as it is for you. I can be patient for as long as necessary." She pulled Alex's head onto her warm breast. "I know everything's going to work out for us, sweetheart."

Alex sighed, her warm breath causing Bryn to involuntarily shudder. "Sometimes I wonder if I'll ever be able to remember why I am the way I am...or if I'll ever be able to let you touch me there..."

Bryn kissed the dark head tenderly. "Give it some time, my love. Bonnie said you're making good progress. You'll see. I promise, we're going to be just fine."

About two o'clock in the morning, Alex awoke from a terrible dream—Bryn had deserted her because of her problems with intimacy. The dark haired woman was in a cold sweat and her heart was pounding violently. She fought down a wave of nausea.

"You'd never do that to me, would you Bryn?" She stroked the sleeping blonde's cheek. "I know you wouldn't...I can feel how much you love me."

Bryn smiled in her sleep. "Mmm," she mumbled.

Alex crept out of bed, putting on her gray boxers and matching gray tee shirt. She went downstairs to the basement, intent on facing the unknown even though the thought absolutely terrified her. She needed to remember not only for herself, but also for Bryn. Taking a bottle of water from the refrigerator, she screwed off the top and drank from it. Then Dr. Alexandra Morgan sat down next to the dreaded boxes, the contents of which she instinctively knew held the key to her past and to her future as well.

Alex opened the last and the largest of the four boxes. She pulled out a bag of smooth, rosy seashells. Pouring the tiny shells into the palm of her hand, she smiled wistfully as she suddenly remembered something that happened late in the summer of 1975.

The tall, handsome surgeon and his raven-haired daughter walked happily, hand in hand along the beach. They both loved the feeling of the smooth, wet sand beneath their bare feet. A cool breeze swept the child's dark bangs across her forehead.

"Do you think she'll like these shells, Dad?" The seven-year-old bent down to pick up a particularly pretty one.

He smiled down at his daughter. She was such a considerate child. "She'll love them, Lex...she loves anything that you give her. The two of you are very special friends."

"Yeah...we'll be best friends till eternity."

The proud father laughed indulgently at his precocious daughter's vocabulary, gently tousling her hair. "If you say so, Lex."

Alex shook her head as her heart pounded wildly.

Who was I gathering shells for? Who did I think would be my best friend till eternity? Bryn's the only real friend I've ever had. Cold sweat beaded above her lip. As Alex trembled uncontrollably, she rummaged through the contents of the box, desperately searching for a clue. Her hands found a yellowed piece of paper that had a name and address on it. Alex's blue eyes grew wide with shock as she read: "Bryn O'Neill, 127 Langham Court, Atlanta, Ga 31529." There was a telephone number listed as well.

Images from the past formed in her mind. Closing her eyes, she tried to control the panic that threatened to overwhelm her, swallowing hard against the bile rising in her throat.

The slender seven-year-old was dressed for bed in her over-sized Snoopy tee shirt. Harry the teddy bear was hidden beneath the covers of her bed. The little girl didn't want him to be discovered and sent back to the top of her mother's closet. She reached under her bed and pulled out a shoebox filled with her special treasures. Carefully opening the box, she took out a slip of paper.

Lexi sat on her bed and reached for the telephone on the nightstand. Just as she started to dial the number written on the paper, her door opened and Olivia stepped into the room. Quickly, she replaced the receiver back in its cradle.

"Alexandra," her mother barked sternly. "Were you about to call Bryn?"

The little girl thought for a moment and then made an important decision. "Mother, I have to call Bryn before I go to sleep. What if she needs me?"

Her blue eyes grew wide with fear. "Or, what if she's died and I don't even know about it. You never let me talk to her." She bravely picked up the receiver again.

"You two can't be friends anymore. Bryn lives too far away. Besides, you're just children. You don't even know what true friendship is."

"But I miss her." The child's lower lip trembled. "And I miss Daddy. I want them back. Please, Mommy?" The blue eyes filled with tears. "Please, please, let me call her. I have to talk to her." She knew she wasn't allowed to cry, but she could no longer control her grief. Lexi sobbed bitterly, never letting go of the receiver. The confusion, rage, and pain of the last six weeks came pouring out of the little girl.

Her mother had no patience for emotional outbursts. "No crying, Alexandra. Give me that phone this instant."

"No!" Lexi screamed, as she stood up on the bed, her fingers clenched tightly around the telephone receiver.

"Give me that phone now." Her mother was furious, shaking with rage. "I want you to forget about Bryn—never mention her name to me again.

"No. I hate you," the child shouted. "I wish you had died instead of Daddy. I hate you so much. I wish I had died, too. Why did my daddy leave me? Why did he leave me with you?" The child's sobs became hysterical.

"I'm all you've got now, so stop crying. And give me that damn phone. You will not call Bryn. Give it to me...right now." She grabbed the phone as Lexi pulled hard in the opposite direction. A loud, sickening pop was heard.

The child fell to the floor, her right arm dangling limply at her side. Lying on the floor in shock and in terrible pain, Lexi's world had completely crumbled.

"Oh, my God. Alexandra. I'm so sorry. I didn't mean to hurt you...it was an accident." She knelt next to the child as her housekeeper came running into the room.

"Olivia. What in God's name have you done to her?" Anna's face was pale with fury. "Isn't it bad enough that you abuse her emotionally?" She rushed to Lexi's side.

"Don't you dare speak to me like that ever again. Besides, it was an accident. I tried to take the phone and she pulled it away. I'm so...so sorry." Olivia started to cry.

The housekeeper gently gathered the trembling child into her arms. "We've got to get her to the hospital right away. You may have dislocated her arm— or worse. Call an ambulance—she looks like she's going into shock."

Once she was safely in Anna's embrace, Lexi whimpered. An agonizing, searing pain cut through her arm and shoulder. But it was nothing compared to the pain in her heart.

Chapter 17

Bryn tried to reach her lover. Alex was drowning in an ocean of tears beyond Bryn's grasp. Each time she held out her hand, something pulled Alex away.

"Bryn...I need you. Please don't leave me." *The blue eyes looked pleadingly into her own.* "Don't go...I need you. Please?" *She held out her hand for Bryn, her voice desperate and haunting.*

"I'm coming, Lex. Just hang on." *Again, Bryn reached out for Alex, but she was yanked away at the last minute.*

Alex was frantic; her blue eyes filled with terror. "Hurry, Bryn...I can't hang on much longer."

Bryn fought with every fiber of her being to reach her soul mate. She pulled forward with all her might and grabbed Alex just as she was about to disappear beneath the surface of the water.

Drenched with perspiration, Bryn awoke with a start. She had managed to rescue Alex in her nightmare, but she knew something was still terribly wrong. Bryn reached out to her lover for comfort, but she wasn't there. Instantly, Bryn knew Alex was in trouble—her heart was telling her that something dreadful had happened.

The blonde jumped out of bed and literally threw on her tank top and boxers. "Where are you, Lex?" she whispered, her voice cracking. Panic stricken, she ran to the basement stairs. As Bryn reached the top step, her heart stopped for a moment. "Oh, dear God."

Lying helpless on the basement floor, Alex was huddled in a corner next to an open box. Shivering uncontrollably, she was unable to cry, scream, or even speak. She needed Bryn more than she had ever needed her before but was powerless to call for help.

"Lex?" Bryn asked gently, fighting back tears as she reached her lover and knelt beside her. "What happened, honey?" Alex stared straight ahead, rubbing her right arm and shoulder as if she were in pain. With a breaking heart, Bryn looked into those tortured blue eyes. "Can you tell me what's wrong?" She gently stroked the dark hair away from her face. "Did you remember something?"

Her lover was unable to answer, so Bryn just gathered her into her arms and rocked her like a child. Alex's skin was ice cold to the touch, and she continued to tremble violently. Realizing that Alex was in shock, Bryn's nursing instincts took over. "Listen to me, sweetheart. I need to get you upstairs and try to get you warm. Can you walk with me?" Bryn gently kissed the top of her head.

Alex nodded, her eyes slowly focusing on Bryn's

face. The petite blonde helped her partner stand up. Fortunately, Bryn's strength far surpassed her size. It was a painfully slow and difficult trek to their upstairs bedroom, but they finally made it. Bryn tucked Alex into their bed and covered her with extra blankets. Then she got in next to her lover and held her as close as possible, rubbing her back and willing warmth and love into the cold, limp body.

"Is that better?" Alex nodded once again, still trembling, still unable to speak. For the first time, Bryn noticed her friend's right hand was balled up in a tight fist. Bryn gently took the hand and rubbed it.

"Honey, you're cutting off the circulation...open your hand, please...just try to relax it." Alex's body refused to cooperate. Bryn carefully pried the slender fingers open, one by one. A yellowed slip of paper was crumpled up in her palm. Turning on the bedside lamp, Bryn took the paper and read it. A loud gasp escaped her lips, and her heart pounded wildly. "Lex? Did you remember me?"

Alex shuddered. At first Bryn thought it was merely the cold, but the shudders grew in intensity, until Alex was struggling to breathe. She was trying to cry, but she couldn't. The pain was too much and she couldn't release it.

"I'm here for you, love," Bryn soothed. "I've got you...everything's gonna be all right. Just let it go. I'll hold you. I promise."

Alex took a deep breath, and the dam burst. She cried as if her heart would break. In Bryn's tender embrace, she finally set free the unspeakable torment she had borne alone for so many years. The young nurse held her tight, giving her love and support throughout the storm. Almost an hour later, Alex gained some measure of composure and was able to offer a halting explanation.

"She wanted...me to...forget you...Bryn. She wouldn't..." Alex hiccupped, "let me...call you...I was afraid...you needed me...I..."

"Take it easy, honey. Stop for a minute and try to get your breath." Bryn rubbed the shaking shoulders, trying to calm her. "Who wouldn't let you? Was it Olivia?"

Alex nodded, sobbing. "She hurt me...just because I wanted to...call you...so I just...I just forgot about you...Oh, God. I'm so sorry, Bryn. I didn't want to forget you. You're my best friend; you're my...my soul mate."

"Dear God. No." Her worst fears had finally been realized. *Please tell me she didn't molest you, Lex,* Bryn silently pleaded. Trembling in fear and anger, she tried to regain her composure for Alex's sake. Taking a deep breath she asked, "Can you tell me how it happened, honey?"

"I can't...not yet...I'm so sorry...sorry I forgot you, Bryn." Alex cried bitter tears of anguish and regret.

"Shh. It's not your fault. You were just a little girl. A scared, confused little girl. But you're not that little girl anymore. Olivia can never hurt you again...or keep us apart. Together, we're stronger than she will ever be." She held Alex close to her breast; the steady beat of her heart calming her soul mate. Her mind in turmoil, Bryn was far from calm. *Lex remembered me.*

About thirty minutes had passed when Bryn made

a decision. Taking a deep breath, she gathered up her courage. "I need to ask you something very important, honey. But if you're not ready to answer, then please let me know."

Alex nodded against Bryn's shoulder.

"When...when you said Olivia hurt you, did you mean she...did she..." Bryn couldn't even say the word aloud.

Alex's face crumpled. "Molest me? No. It wasn't anything like that." Suddenly angry, the surgeon sat up and buried her face in her hands. "That bitch just dislocated my arm, that's all...tearing a ligament in the process. The injury was so severe, that it required surgery. I'm damn lucky that it didn't affect my whole, fucking career." Alex got off the bed to pace around the room, her face ashen and drawn. She ripped off her tee shirt, pointing to a thin, white scar on her shoulder. "You ever wonder how I got this?" She took a deep shuddering breath. "Well, I'll tell you. My loving mother gave this to me!" Alex burst into angry tears, raging. "I've never hated anyone so much in my whole life. I'm full of hatred, Bryn. I'm eaten up with it, and it completely consumes me. It's no wonder I'm unable to accept your love." The distraught woman slowly dropped to the floor, weeping bitterly.

Bryn knelt by her side and placed Alex's head in her lap, tenderly stroking her hair. "Lex, I love you. I can't even begin to tell you how much. I'm so sorry Olivia hurt you...I'll never understand how a mother could do that to her own child." Bryn leaned over to kiss the dark head. "But...I believe in you. You're strong enough to conquer your fears and come to terms with the terrible things that happened to you when you were little. And, you won't have to do it alone...we will get through this together. You know how precious you are to me. I will never hurt you and I'll help you every step of the way. I give you my word.

"Lex, you have such a marvelous capacity for love. I saw it when we were girls and I see it now. I see it every single day of my life with you. You've always been able to love, you just never knew it." Bryn paused, wiping tears from Alex's cheek. "There's only one way to get past this terrible pain. I know how hard it'll be for you, but you won't have to do it alone. I think you need to forgive your mother. It's the only way you can finally put this behind you."

In the darkest night of her life, Alex's soul was drowning in a sea of pain, fear, and anger. With Bryn's love reaching out and rescuing her, Alex could finally see the light at the end of the tunnel...and Bryn was that light.

Chapter 18

Bryn struggled to awaken fully. She rolled over, glancing at the bedside clock. "Two o'clock," she groaned. "I've never slept this late in my life." Once her mind became fully cognizant, she remembered the hellish night before. Alex lay next to her, apparently in a very deep sleep. Her lover's face was extremely pale, and her eyes were swollen and puffy. Bryn's heart contracted painfully as she thought about all that Alex had been through. "Everything's going to work out fine, Lex," she whispered, kissing the surgeon's forehead tenderly. "I love you."

A faint smile crossed Alex's face, and she snuggled closer to Bryn. "Don't get up, Bryn," she murmured hoarsely. "Stay with me."

"Honey, I would, but my bladder's about to burst. I'll be right back." The blonde climbed out of bed and went to the blue and white tiled bathroom.

"Come back soon," Alex mumbled sleepily. "I'm

so cold."

In a few minutes, Bryn slid back into bed next to her partner. "You're still cold?" she asked, pulling Alex close. "My God. You are. You've been freezing all night long. Are you sure you're okay?"

"Yeah...I think so. I was so upset last night, I must have gone into shock...I guess my system kind of shut down." Alex shivered.

"Well, then, let's warm you up. How 'bout some coffee? I know I could sure use some."

"Yeah...coffee sounds good. But, please hurry back...I don't want to be alone."

"C'mon, then." Bryn tugged on Alex's arm gently. "I'll make you a bed on the couch out on the porch. You'll be right next to me while I'm in the kitchen." Bryn knew how the screened in porch seemed to soothe Alex's soul.

Alex smiled. "I'd like that very much."

Bryn brewed coffee after Alex was settled comfortably on the couch, wrapped in several warm blankets.

When Bryn returned to the porch, the surgeon sat up and motioned for Bryn to sit next to her. Looking at the tray, Alex smiled at the chocolate crumb donuts, a favorite of hers. "Thanks, Bryn. This looks great, but I'm not sure if I can keep anything down right now. The coffee will have to tide me over for a while."

"Lexi, you can't eat?" Concerned, Bryn laid her hand on Alex's forehead.

The surgeon raised an eyebrow at the term of endearment. "I'm not really ill, Squeak. It's just..." Alex took a deep breath and blew it out slowly.

"Right now, I have these images in my head...of Olivia...dislocating my arm, tearing the ligament...and...and it just makes me feel sick to my stomach." Alex sipped her coffee, desperately wanting to change the subject.

Bryn took the coffee mug from Alex and set it on the table beside her. She wrapped her arms around her soul mate as tightly as she could. "Somehow, we're gonna make it through this weekend, my love. If you need me to, I'll sit with you, hold you, listen to you, and talk to you every second till Monday morning comes...I promise. I think you'll feel much better once you get everything off your chest. Okay?"

"Okay. Bryn...thank you for finding me last night. I don't know how you knew I needed you, but I'm just so glad you did. It couldn't have been easy for you."

Bryn sighed, lacing her fingers with her lover's. "I don't know how I knew you were in trouble, either, Lex. Somehow, I just knew. And yes, it was really hard. I was so scared. For a minute there, I thought I might lose you."

Alex wiped away the tears that fell down Bryn's cheeks. "I'm going to be all right. Last night was the beginning of my recovery from this nightmare. It was terrifying—but bearable, because you were there for me when I needed you—just like you always are." The dark brows furrowed in pain. "When I was lying on that cold floor, I thought I was dying emotionally...and then, my angel showed up. I've never been so glad to see anyone in my whole life. Bryn...I...I was so afraid. I really thought I was gonna lose it there."

With a sad smile, Alex pulled her soul mate into her arms. "You know, it's a miracle that after all these years, I finally remembered my one real friend. I just can't believe I found you again." Alex kissed Bryn tenderly, putting all her heart and soul into the kiss. She felt great comfort with the knowledge that the Bryn she loved so much now was the cherished friend she had adored as a child. She hoped that their love would see her through her devastating memories—memories of a woman who could do so much emotional and physical damage to her own child.

After the kiss ended, Bryn took Alex's face in her hands, peering into the deep blue eyes. A look of concern crossed her face. "Your eyes look pretty swollen, honey. Why don't you lie down and let me put some cold compresses on them?"

"That's okay, Squeak. No one will see them but you and you love me no matter what. Right?"

"Oh, you are so right. Besides, you always look beautiful to me, Lex."

Alex gave her companion a huge bear hug. Bryn smiled, patting the surgeon's hand. "You give the best hugs, Lex. Just like when we were little. Can you remember those hugs?"

Alex smiled wistfully, nodding. "I do recall being very afraid of hurting you after your surgery. You looked so small in that big hospital bed."

A small, golden haired girl lay propped up against a mountain of soft pillows. Bryn hugged a stuffed, brown dog close to her bandaged chest. Tears rolled down her cheeks, dripping onto the dog's soft fur. Kathleen O'Neill was frustrated by her inability to make her only child smile. She turned away from the bed, so that Bryn would not see the tears in her own eyes.

At that moment, the door swung open, and the unhappy child's best friend bounced into the room. Bryn's mother breathed a huge sigh of relief.

"Bryn!" Lexi called happily. She hurried to the little girl's bedside and carefully climbed up on a chair—after removing her sneakers first. Her big blue eyes were immediately sad at the sight of her friend crying. She touched a finger to Bryn's cheek, gently wiping a tear away. "What's the matter, Bryn?" Her lip poked out ever so slightly in sympathy.

"Lexi," Bryn cried pathetically. "I was missing you, and they pulled a tube out of my hand. It...it really hurt. I wanna go home...and I want you to come with me. Please, Lexi." The child's sobs grew louder. Upset that her normally brave little girl was so distraught, Mrs. O'Neill moved toward the bed to comfort her daughter, but stopped. Lexi was giving Bryn all the support and the love necessary.

"Shh, Bryn. You'll feel better soon." The older girl hugged her little friend carefully, tenderly patting her back. "You have to stay here to get well. You won't have to have any more surgery, and the worst part is over. You'll see. And I promise I'll come see you every day. Okay?"

Sniffling, Bryn nodded her head slightly.

"Want me to get you some ice cream?"

The little blonde nodded again, this time very enthusiastically. Her usually sunny disposition was quickly returning.

"Great...I'll get some for both of us, then." Lexi confidently pushed the call button as if she owned the hospital. Bryn reached for her friend's hand and held it tight. She felt so lucky to have someone as special as Lexi for a best friend.

The two women gazed at one another, both reveling in the shared memory. Sighing deeply, Bryn wiped tears from her eyes. "You'll never know what your friendship meant to me then...and what it means to me now." She squeezed the surgeon's hand.

"Oh, I think I know, Bryn. I know." Alex leaned her head against Bryn's.

"What do you think bound us so closely together? I mean, we were just little girls...but there was something so special between us."

Alex sighed. "You promise not to laugh at me?" she asked hesitantly.

"Of course not." Bryn kissed Alex's palm. She loved the surgeon's strong, beautiful hands.

"Well...I believe we were always meant to be together...I never truly cared about anyone until I met you."

Bryn's whole face lit up. "I've thought that, too, but I wasn't sure how to tell you. I can't remember a time when I didn't love you."

Alex smiled wistfully. "Same here. I think we really are soul mates, bonded together forever...and somehow, we knew it even as children."

Bryn laid her head on Alex's strong shoulder. No more words were necessary.

****

Bryn carried the breakfast tray back into the kitchen. Alex drank her coffee, but she was unable to eat any of the delicious doughnuts. Her lover wasn't surprised. The lack of appetite when she was upset was a common reaction for Alex. Even when things were going well, she was burdened with a sensitive stomach. Bryn, on the other hand, could always eat.

The blonde put the dishes in the dishwasher and yawned. She felt tired and drained, and she was still concerned about Alex. The surgeon was so emotionally and physically exhausted, that she could barely keep her eyes open. *Maybe I can persuade Lex to go back to bed,* Bryn thought to herself. She chuckled aloud thinking how stubborn her partner could be at times. "Maybe if I offer to go with her..."

As Bryn entered the porch, she felt a deep pang in her heart at the sight before her. Alex was curled up on the couch sound asleep, something she rarely did. Bryn plucked an afghan from the back of the couch and covered her up, then leaned over and kissed the smooth forehead. "I hope all your dreams are sweet from now on, my love."

****

The blonde somehow managed to unlock the door to the side entrance with her arms full. She set down the bags of Chinese food, along with her keys, on the tiled counter. Slipping out of her brown suede jacket, she went to the hall closet and carefully hung the jacket on a hanger. Neatness was a trait she and Alex had in common.

Turning back towards the kitchen, Bryn peeked out onto the porch. She expected to see Alex still sleeping soundly, but the couch was empty. "Lex?" Bryn called, heading into the bedroom.

Alex, freshly showered and dressed in a white oxford shirt and tight fitting jeans, stepped out of the bathroom. Her long hair was wet and combed back from her forehead. The beautiful surgeon's natural tan color had returned, and her eyes had lost their puffiness. As soon as Bryn saw her lover, the Chinese food was temporarily forgotten. Images of a naked Alex lying under her flitted through her mind and she had to restrain herself from throwing Lex on the bed and ripping off her clothes. Regaining control of her libido, Bryn gathered her up in a tender, loving hug instead.

"God, you look so much better. How are you feeling?"

Alex returned the affectionate gesture warmly. "I feel a lot better. I guess I slept all day." The surgeon played with Bryn's golden hair. "What about you, Squeak?" she asked, concern in her voice. "Did you take a nap?"

"Yeah...I did. Then I got up, took a shower, and went out for a couple of videos and Chinese food. I ordered all your favorites, too."

Alex buried her nose in Bryn's fragrant golden hair, inhaling deeply. "Mmm...I thought I smelled something good...but it doesn't smell half as good as you do." She nibbled the blonde's soft ear.

Bryn tried to ignore the heat spreading though her body and concentrated on what was best for Alex.

"Lex, sweetheart...listen...you need to eat something first. You haven't had anything since last night...Ooo, stop that," she pleaded breathlessly. "I can't think."

Alex moved her tongue along her lover's neckline. "I was planning on eating something," she promised, in a deep, low tone. "But it's not Chinese, and it's definitely not take out."

"Oh, God." Bryn's body melted into her lover's strong arms, as they both fell onto the huge sleigh bed.

Some time later, they lay together, holding and caressing one another. Bryn thought about how much she wanted to touch Alex. How much she wanted to give the same pleasure she had just received. Tonight Alex didn't even seem to desire her own sexual gratification—she made no attempt to bring herself to orgasm. The blonde suspected that Alex was feeling more than a little uncomfortable masturbating in front of her. Bryn wanted to help in any way she could, but Alex's emotions were still too raw after last night. She didn't want to push her lover in any way at this critical point in their relationship. *If Lex can open up more about what happened to her when she was a child, maybe she'll be able to accept my love,* Bryn thought hopefully.

Alex kissed the golden head tenderly. Bryn, using the surgeon's soft, right breast as a pillow, was too content to move an inch. "Lex," she whispered, "you are so incredible. I think I'll keep you."

Alex flushed with pleasure as long fingers traced soothing patterns on Bryn's behind. "I have to keep my best girl happy now, don't I? And speaking of happy, maybe we should get dressed and find that

Chinese food. Your stomach is making an awful racket."

Bryn swatted her lover playfully. "Go ahead. Make fun of me."

Alex chuckled, planting another kiss on the top of Bryn's head.

The two women put on their favorite boxer shorts and tee shirts, and went into the kitchen. After piling their plates high with food, they took the plates, along with bottles of Snapple and Coors Lite, out to the porch. Bryn silently hoped that her soul mate would be able to eat.

"This is great, Bryn." Alex dug into the Hunan dish with her chopsticks, biting into a plump shrimp.

"I thought you'd enjoy it, honey. How's your stomach feeling?"

"Much better." Alex took a bite of fried rice. "You know, it's starting to sink in that I can finally remember you. I feel really good about that, even though those memories include a lot of terrible things."

"Lex, my love...don't forget, I'll be here for you anytime you want to talk." Bryn cupped Alex's cheek in her hand.

"I know, Squeak...thank you. I don't think I could ever tell anyone but you." Alex intertwined her fingers with Bryn's. "I trust you with all·my heart."

After dinner, Bryn put a tray with two mugs of hot chocolate on the bedside stand while Alex loaded a tape of an old horror movie into the VCR. Bryn propped two pillows against the headboard and sat upright in the bed. Alex climbed in and lay between her legs, her back against Bryn's chest, with the blonde's arms wrapped snugly around her. Usually this position was reversed, but Alex was in need of extra cuddling.

They were half way through the movie when Alex turned to look at Bryn. "Why didn't my mother love me?" she asked, in a voice so small and vulnerable. "Did I do something wrong?"

Bryn thought her heart would shatter into a million pieces. She hugged Alex tighter, planting a kiss on her neck. "You think she didn't love you, sweetheart?"

Alex trembled violently. "Of course not. She was so angry with me that she dislocated my arm and tore a ligament. And, why? Because I wanted to call my best friend. On top of that, she lied to me. I was too devastated to remember the accident. So when I asked her what happened, she told me I did it sliding down the banister of the staircase. Like a fool, I believed her, too." Alex took a deep shuddering breath. "Why wouldn't I believe her? She *was* my mother. Mothers don't lie to their kids about things like that—no mother who loves her child would do that. But, mine did—that bitch. She's nothing but a liar...a fucking liar. And I hate her...Goddamn her. I hate her, Bryn."

Bryn rubbed Alex's arms and held her tight. She would help her partner get through another painful, emotional storm, but the devastation to her lover's soul could not heal overnight. "I know you hate her, honey. I don't blame you, but you need to try and let go of the hate. Just keep talking to me...I'm here."

"I...I was so scared, and the pain was excruciating. Anna rode in the ambulance and tried her best to comfort me." Alex swallowed the lump in her throat. "You know, Olivia didn't even come with me. How could she do that, Bryn? How could she just let me go to the hospital without her? I was just a little girl. I needed my mother...and she wasn't there. But then, why would she come? She wasn't a real mother. I never had one. All I had was a self-centered bitch who hurt me and lied to me." Alex's voice trailed off as she murmured, "She never loved me, she never loved me..."

"Keep talking to me, honey. I'm listening." Bryn kept up a steady stream of hugs and caresses, offering all the emotional support Alex craved.

"It was David who Olivia loved—it was never me. She didn't hurt him...there was no emotional abuse directed at David, just me. Although, I have to admit, she did ignore him sometimes and manipulated him." Alex laughed bitterly. "He's probably only half as fucked up as I am," she spat.

"Lex, for God's sake." Almost choking on the words, Bryn stammered, "You're not...fucked up. You're hurt, angry, and confused. But you're going to get through this. I'll help you. I promise, my love."

"Will I, Bryn? Will I ever be able to allow you to make love to me, like a normal person would? I wanted to tonight. You don't know how much I wanted it. I'm totally overwhelmed by my need to have you touch me in every way imaginable. I...I need to feel you inside of me..." Alex struggled to maintain her composure. "But, damn it, I can't let you. Do you know how inadequate that makes me feel?" Sad blue eyes filled with tears.

"It must be so hard for you, honey...I can't even

imagine. But I believe you will...very soon. And even if it never happens, it doesn't really matter to me. All that I'll ever care about is that you love me. Don't you know that by now?" Bryn's voice cracked and she cried as if her heart would break.

Alex couldn't bear it. She held onto her lover as if her life depended on it—and in reality, it did. Bryn's tears caused that seemingly impenetrable barrier to Alex's soul to finally shatter. Clinging to one another, they cried together until all their tears were spent.

Finally, Alex was able to tell Bryn in graphic detail about that terrible night—the pain, the fear, the horror, and worst of all, the knowledge that her own mother hurt her. And how, even though Alex had no memory of the accident and accepted her mother's explanation, their relationship continued to disintegrate until there was nothing left but hatred.

The pale seven-year-old slept peacefully, still under sedation. Anna leaned over her bed, stroking the child's beautiful raven hair tenderly. An I.V. line dripped nourishment into a vein in her slender left arm. A heavy cast encased her right arm from her hand to her shoulder.

Anna sat down in a big, comfortable rocking chair next to young Lexi's bed. She had requested that the chair be moved into the child's hospital room so she could rock the little girl once she awakened from surgery. Lexi would need as much emotional support as she could possibly get.

Long, dark lashes fluttered, and the child slowly opened her eyes. "Daddy?" she whispered hoarsely.

"Hi, sweetheart. It's Anna...I'm here for you. How are you feeling?" she crooned. Anna leaned over and kissed Lexi's wan cheek.

"My arm...it hurts." The child appeared confused. "Anna, what happened to me?"

"You don't remember?"

"No." Her breathing increased, and she started to perspire.

"We'll talk about this later, honey. Just rest now." She pulled Lexi close.

The child looked around anxiously. "Is Mommy here?"

"No, sweetheart. She's at home with Davy."

"Then...is it okay if I cry?" she asked in a small voice, her lip trembling.

"Yes, Lexi...it's okay to cry." Being careful of her cast and I.V., Anna gently lifted the little girl from her bed. She sat down in the rocking chair with her and rocked, humming softly.

The child cried quietly into Anna's sturdy shoulder. Soon, a nurse appeared, and injected pain medicine into Lexi's I.V. She drifted off into a dreamless sleep, clinging to the kind woman who had cared for her since she was only two days old. Anna would keep the bright light in Lexi's soul from being extinguished completely.

Bryn listened to every word intently, comforting Alex in a way that no other human being could. She reassured her continually, provided plenty of hugs, and offered total, unconditional love. Her efforts were just what the doctor ordered. After almost a lifetime of nightmares, Alex was able to find a peaceful sleep—her heart purged at last of the deepest pain imaginable.

Chapter 19

The petite blonde awakened slowly. Someone was lovingly caressing her face with long, slender fingers. "Wake up, Squeak, I've got your favorite pastries here," Alex teased in a singsong voice. Bryn smiled and stretched, making her trademark 'squeaking' sound. The surgeon chuckled. "C'mon, or I'll start without you...and you know there won't be any blueberry croissants left if I do."

"Huh?" Bryn sat upright in bed rubbing eyes that were as swollen and red as her partner's. "I'm awake now," Bryn yawned. "Where are the pastries?"

Alex smirked as she set a tray across Bryn's lap. "Here you go, Squeak...There's freshly brewed Kona coffee with two sugars and lots of half and half; blueberry, strawberry, and raspberry croissants—all with cream cheese, and the latest issue of Baseball Weekly. How's that for service?"

"This is wonderful, Lex. Thank you." She gave

her soul mate an affectionate hug. Bryn positively beamed with relief. More than once, Bryn had been truly frightened for her lover during the last thirty-six hours. Yet, here the surgeon was, going on with her life and even treating Bryn to a special breakfast in bed. It was obvious to Bryn that Alex was still emotionally exhausted, but her features seemed more relaxed, and unbelievably, she even looked younger.

Alex sat down next to Bryn, and took a bite of blueberry croissant, followed by a sip of coffee. *I can't remember the last time anything tasted this wonderful—and what happened to that persistent pain in my stomach? It's gone.*

Bryn smiled at her lover, cupping her cheek in her hand. "You look like you feel pretty good today, Lex. Did talking about things last night help?"

"Yeah...it must have, because for the first time since I can remember, I don't have this nagging ache in my gut." The surgeon laid a hand across her stomach. "It feels great."

Bryn gave Alex an affectionate squeeze. "I'm so happy for you, Lex. But if you don't stop eating up all my croissants, you're going to have a different kind of stomach ache." The blonde slowly moved her hand to the last blueberry pastry, intent on making it hers.

"Oh, no, you don't." Alex grabbed the favored pastry, and started to stuff it into her mouth. At the last minute she grinned and divided it in two, giving half to Bryn.

"Thanks for sharing, Lex. You're the best." Bryn leaned over for a kiss.

When the kiss ended, Alex gave Bryn her heart

stopping, lopsided smile. "I'll always share with you...you own my heart...forever."

* * * * * * * * *

The two women spent the rest of the weekend recuperating, and were able to fully enjoy their time together. Alex seemed more relaxed to Bryn; her beautiful face unmarred by the usual tension. The blonde was especially delighted to see an increase in her lover's appetite. She had always thought that Alex was too thin, and hoped her improved eating habits might cause a weight gain.

Hmmm...relaxed, actually hungry once in a while, playful—I wonder if these little changes might carry over into another area of our life. Maybe Lex will finally be able to let me love her. It might just happen if I give her a gentle push. No...not a good plan, Bryn. She's always so skittish, even when we talk about it. Lex has to be the one to decide when the right time will be.

Sunday evening found the lovers in bed. Bryn sat behind Alex and held her in such a way that she could kiss her ears and neck and caress her breasts. This enabled Alex to masturbate while enjoying the intense pleasure she received from Bryn's touch. During their previous lovemaking sessions, the surgeon would never allow Bryn's hand to wander below her navel. Tonight Alex let the blonde stroke her lower belly. When Bryn's left hand accidentally grazed soft, dark curls, Alex was immediately sent over the edge. Bryn was so moved and aroused that she joined her.

They lay quietly for several minutes—each one trying to get her ragged breathing under control. Alex was the first to speak. Half laughing and half crying, she wiped tears from her eyes. "Bryn, you're turning me into a leaky faucet. That was unbelievable."

Bryn rolled on top of her lover for a deep, searing kiss. "Oh, Lex, believe it. You almost let me touch you, and you didn't panic."

Alex chuckled. "Well, that definitely wasn't a panic response. And it felt so good. Come here, you." Alex returned the kiss, tenderly stroking Bryn's long, golden hair. Then she flipped her soul mate over and showed her just how much she loved her—twice.

****

Alex sat quietly; head bowed, staring at her hands. She loathed discussing her personal life with anyone except Bryn. Now, she was forced to discuss the most intimate details of her life with a professional—someone whose job it was to probe and analyze. Only her deep love for Bryn enabled her to reveal so much about herself to her therapist.

Dr. Bonnie Kaplan's blue eyes showed warmth and caring. "Here is what I suggest, Alex. Allow Bryn to touch you while you are making love. If something comes of it, fantastic. But, if you can't reach a climax, then try again another time. Don't sell Bryn short...she'll understand. In all my years as a therapist, I have never met a more loving and compassionate partner. Please try. You have made wonderful progress. The only thing holding you back from full recovery is your fear."

Alex sighed deeply. "I want to, more than anything I've ever wanted in my life. I crave her touch. And I have been trying. Just last night, I thought I might be ready but I couldn't get any further than letting Bryn stroke my lower abdomen." Alex looked down at her hands. "I know you're right...I'm afraid. Before I met Bryn, I had given up on having a sex life. It was so humiliating not ever being able to reach a climax...not to mention frustrating. It ruined every relationship I ever had. But with Bryn, it would be much worse. If I failed with her...I...I don't think I could survive it."

"You've already leaped over a very big hurdle, Alex. As your therapist, I think you're ready for the next jump. But it has to be your decision. I would never insist upon it."

"I appreciate that. But what if it never happens? What if I can never let Bryn touch me? How will she feel? Why would she even want to stay with someone like me—an emotional cripple?" Alex buried her face in her hands. "And in any event, I don't deserve her love. Bryn is such a wonderful person. She would never have had an abortion—no matter what the circumstances. I worry about my deficiencies all the time, and it really bothers me. Bryn should have nothing but the best, and I'm a far cry from that."

Bonnie's heart went out to the younger woman. "We've been through all this time and again, Alex. Bryn is a grown woman who knows her own mind. And she has made her decision. She adores you, you know." Bonnie stood up and sat next to her pensive patient. "What's really going on here, Alex? Please share it with me. I'm here to help you."

The surgeon shrugged. "I don't know."

Bonnie patted her patient's shoulder. "Okay, Alex. Think about what I've said, and we'll talk about it tomorrow. And please, give Bryn my regards."

****

Later that evening, Alex paced nervously on the enclosed porch of her home. "Where is she, and why isn't she answering her cell phone?" She sat down in a chair on the porch and attempted to read the latest journal of *Pediatric Cardiology*. Too worried to concentrate, she tossed it aside, staring out the window while she drank her second bottle of Coor's Lite.

Just after nine o'clock, a car pulled into the driveway. Alex knew from the sound of the engine that it was Bryn. She hurried to the front door and opened it to an exhausted, hungry, and very irritable blonde. Expecting a little sympathy from her soul mate, Bryn got the third degree instead.

"Where in hell have you been, and why didn't you call me, or answer your cell phone?" the surgeon asked furiously, her face pale.

Bryn's green eyes flashed with anger. "Look Alex, first of all, I was stuck in traffic behind a horrible accident. Second, I accidentally left my cell phone in my work locker. So I couldn't call you or answer your damn call, Dr. Cranky. And third, fourth, fifth, and sixth: my head hurts. I'm tired, I haven't eaten since noon, and if you don't mind, I have to go pee right now." The petite blonde stalked off in a huff.

Alex was chagrined, but her feelings were hurt, too. She wasn't accustomed to Bryn yelling at her. Sighing, she retreated to the porch. When provoked, her sweet tempered partner was a real spitfire, and Alex knew when to back off.

Ten minutes later, Bryn stepped out onto the porch. She had changed into a tee shirt and boxers, and had a cold bottle of Snapple in her hand. Alex was sitting on the blue and white loveseat, looking contrite. "I'm really sorry I acted like such an ass, Squeak. I was afraid that something terrible had happened to you. Forgive me?"

Bryn threw herself into her partner's arms, and positioned herself on her lap. They hugged each other tight, soaking up all the love and warmth each had to offer. "Of course, I forgive you, Lex. I'm sorry that you were so worried."

"It's not your fault, Bryn. I don't know what's the matter with me. To tell you the truth, I'm afraid of...losing you. What we have seems too good to be true." Alex gave Bryn another squeeze.

"You had a right to be worried about me when I was late. I probably would have reacted the same way." She stroked Alex's cheek. "But, Lex...I'm not going anywhere, and nothing's going to happen to me. You deserve to be happy...we both deserve to be happy. And anyway, aren't you happy now? I know that my life has never been better—now that you're back in it."

Alex smiled sheepishly. "You're right, Bryn. I've never felt this complete. Right now I'm just feeling a little embarrassed about overreacting."

"Don't be...it just shows me how much you love me." She gave Alex a big kiss on the forehead. "Now, where's the number to Sam's New York Pizza? You must be hungry and I'm famished."

Alex smiled, relieved that Bryn wasn't angry with her. "I'll look it up, Squeak. Want me to rub your shoulders while we wait for dinner?"

Bryn laughed. "You really know the way to a girl's heart."

"Just one heart...the only one that matters."

****

That night, after dinner, Alex and Bryn continued their conversation concerning Alex's fears. Prior to their argument, it had never occurred to Bryn that Alex feared losing her. In retrospect, it made perfect sense. Lex's beloved father died suddenly and unexpectedly. At about the same time, little four-year-old Bryn—her dearest friend—had disappeared from her life. No wonder she worried about losing her partner. Bryn did everything in her power to comfort Lex, and by the time they went to bed, the surgeon was reassured that Bryn would never leave her willingly. As she drifted off to sleep, Alex realized that she was one step closer to healing.

****

The petite nurse cuddled the fussy infant, crooning to him. She had tried everything she could think of to soothe him, but he was missing his mother. Exhausted, and worried about her son, Bryn had persuaded her patient's tired mother to go to the cafeteria for a cup of coffee and a bite to eat.

"How about a story?" Bryn adjusted the baby's oxygen mask, which was making him even fussier. He looked into Bryn's face with big blue eyes as she stroked his silky black hair. "You are one cute kid, Riley James Smith," she whispered in a soft voice. "You kind of remind me of someone special I know." The infant cooed, unable to resist his nurse's magical way with children. She hugged him close to her breast. "Now, on to my story."

"Can anyone listen in?" Alex stuck her head in the door, her beautiful face and smile lighting up the room.

Bryn was rocking Riley in a big rocking chair, rubbing soothing circles on his back. "In your case, I'll make an exception. Ordinarily, I'd say no— unless you're sick and cranky." The blonde's green eyes sparkled with mischief.

"For all the attention he's getting, that could be arranged." The surgeon grinned crookedly.

Bryn smirked. "Are we feeling a bit jealous, Dr. Morgan?"

Alex feigned a pout. "Just a bit."

The blonde nurse laughed. "Don't worry, I'll make it up to you later." Then, under her breath she whispered, "spoiled brat."

Alex, who had resumed her professional demeanor, moved closer to examine the baby. Placing the earpiece of her stethoscope into her ears, she murmured, "I heard that."

Bryn just smiled, and then positioned Riley so that Alex could examine him easily. The surgeon was very slow and gentle in her approach, not wanting to make her tiny patient cry. He looked up at Alex with wide, trusting blue eyes as she listened to his heart and checked his vital signs. After completing the examination, the surgeon stood up, her face a mask. Bryn was not fooled; she knew that Alex's expression meant Riley was in trouble.

"What's wrong, Lex?"

"His heart's working really hard—and he's not even feeding or crying. The sooner I repair it, the better. I'm going to schedule him for surgery right away. I can't wait until after Thanksgiving. If I do, he could go into Congestive Heart Failure. I'm sorry, but we may need to postpone our trip to the cottage."

"That's okay. You know I don't mind." Bryn carefully put the baby back in his crib. "His parents are really scared, Lex. They lost their first son to the same heart defect."

"I know. I'll try and reassure them. If we can just get him through surgery, his prognosis is very good. I'll see you tonight." Alex took Riley's chart and brushed two fingers to her lips, turning them towards Bryn as she left the room.

****

Dr. Morgan sat at her desk, facing Alison and Chad Smith, Riley's mother and father. The first meeting with the parents of a patient was always difficult for Alex. She had to be gentle, yet frank with them about their baby's condition.

"As you know, the Balloon Atrial Septostomy performed on Riley at your local hospital was a temporary measure. It was necessary to improve his oxygen supply and to stabilize him. The next procedure is a far more complicated surgery to correct his problem—specifically, an Arterial Switch Operation." Dr. Morgan took a deep breath. "I can only imagine how painful this is for you, but I need to ask you a question. Did your other son have an Arterial Switch Operation?"

The pretty young woman dabbed at her eyes with a tissue. "No, we weren't aware of this surgery when our first son, Robert, was born. But this time, Riley's cardiologist, Dr. Cardin, suggested that we bring him to Atlanta. Dr. Cardin said the latest procedures were being done here, and that you were the best pediatric heart surgeon on the staff of this hospital." She paused, trying to compose herself. "Dr. Morgan, we can't have any more children. With Robert gone, Riley is our only hope. We can't lose Riley...we just can't. He's our whole world." Tears streamed down Alison Smith's face as her husband tried to comfort her.

Alex felt deep sympathy for the young couple. She handed over a box of tissues and waited for the young mother to calm down. "I'm sure you understand that I can't make guarantees, but I don't believe Riley will die. As you already know, Transposition of the Great Arteries is a very serious defect. But, I've done a number of these surgeries, and as of today, my mortality rate is zero." Alex took out a diagram of Riley's defect, using a pencil as a pointer. "With your permission, we'll put him on a heart-lung machine, and open his chest. Then I'll switch the incorrect positions of his pulmonary artery and aorta. I'll also free his coronary arteries, then connect them back to the aorta, using very delicate, hair-thin sutures." Alex smiled warmly. "If all goes well, and I suspect it will, he can even play shortstop on a Little League team someday—if he wants to, and can lead a completely normal life." Dr. Morgan paused. "Of course, any surgery carries risks; particularly heart surgery. But he's in a wonderful facility, and I have a lot of experience with this procedure. If the operation goes well, Riley's long term prognosis is excellent."

Riley's father cleared his throat. "There may be a problem financially, Dr. Morgan. Our first son's hospital bills were staggering, even with insurance. We will pay every dime, but it may take a while."

"Dr. Cardin explained your situation to me...and I've decided to waive my fee."

The young couple was stunned. "But...how can we ever repay you?" they asked in unison.

"You can send me a picture of your happy, healthy son. He's quite a handsome little guy. And very soon, his color will be nice and pink, instead of blue." Alex paused, as she steepled her fingers. "I've scheduled the surgery for tomorrow morning instead of next week. The sooner I correct his problem, the better the outcome for Riley. You should also know that I am planning to be at Cape Cod for Thanksgiving weekend. I'll leave Riley in the very capable hands of Dr. Stephanie Moore. She'll be assisting me during surgery, and she's an excellent doctor. However, if there are any post-op complications, I'll delay my trip."

"Thank you, Dr. Morgan. You have no idea what your kindness means to us." Chad and Alison Smith stood up to leave, but stopped to embrace Alex first.

Even though the surgeon was uncomfortable with public displays of affection, she shyly returned the hugs.

After Riley's parents left her office, Alex wondered why they had made such a fuss—unknowingly embarrassing her. *It's only money, what's the big deal?* As always, Alex thought nothing of her generosity; it was second nature to her. Oddly enough, it didn't dawn on her that most doctors wouldn't have treated the Smiths in such a caring way, let alone waive their fees.

Chapter 20

C'mon, c'mon, c'mon, c'mon now,
Touch me, babe, Can't you see that I am not afraid
What was that promise that you made,
Why won't you tell me what she said
What was that promise that she made
Now I'm gonna love you till the heavens stop the rain
I'm gonna love you till the stars fall from the sky
For you and I...

Dr. Alexandra Morgan arched her neck. After being in surgery for six hours, her legs ached, and her eyes burned from the strain. The Arterial Switch operation required incredible skill and dexterity. Fortunately, Riley James Smith couldn't have been in better hands.

"How's he doing, Sam?" Alex asked the handsome, graying anesthesiologist.

"His vital signs are stable." The doctor chuckled

for a moment. "He's doing fine, Dr. Alex—but I'm not so sure about his anesthesiologist. After all, I'm the one that has to listen to your loud music. What was the name of that singer again?"

Alex mock glared at Dr. Sam Schaeffer. "It's Jim Morrison and the Doors." She sighed. "I'll let that slide this time, Sam. But only because you're such a damned good anesthesiologist." A hint of a smile was evident in the crinkle around Alex's crystal blue eyes. Dr. Morgan still had the capacity to be the "Ice Princess," but now, due to Bryn's loving influence, some of the staff who worked with her could see a thawing of that ice.

The tall surgeon put in the last of the miniscule sutures around Riley's tiny heart, and sighed. "Okay, start warming him up and take him off bypass." Crucial moments passed as they all waited. Slowly, Riley's heart beat strongly on its own. A cheer went up around the operating theatre.

"Close him up for me, Stephanie. Riley's parents are waiting for some good news." Alex couldn't remember when she had been this happy. A difficult operation had been completed without a hitch, and the next thing on her agenda was a long, relaxing weekend with Bryn at their Cape Cod cottage.

Once outside the operating room, the surgeon removed her gloves, cap, and mask, and washed her hands. She then hurried to the family waiting area. Alex walked towards Riley's parents with a smile on her face. "The operation went very well. Riley will be moved to Intensive Care soon, and then you can go in to see him. I expect a complete recovery. As I told you, I'm going to Boston for Thanksgiving. Dr.

Stephanie Moore will see to Riley's progress while I'm gone. I have complete faith in her, and in Riley's determination to get well."

Chad and Alison Smith cried with relief, hugging each other. "Thank you, Dr. Morgan," they both exclaimed. "We'll never be able to thank you enough." Tears ran down Alison Smith's face as she turned to embrace the tall surgeon. "You're a wonderful doctor—and a special person."

Alex smiled shyly. She wasn't comfortable with praise, even from Bryn. "Thank you, Mrs. Smith. Happy Thanksgiving." As she turned to go, Alex paused. "By the way, Riley's nice and pink now."

As she walked down the hall, Alex marveled at the delight she felt in helping Riley and his parents. She had always found her work supremely gratifying, but somehow this was different. She decided it must be because she was beginning to feel complete and whole for the first time since she could remember.

****

The petite blonde closed the latch on her suitcase. Everything was all packed and ready to go. If young Riley Smith continued to do well, Alex and Bryn would be on a plane headed for Boston by seven o'clock tomorrow morning.

Bryn placed her suitcase in the corner next to Alex's bag. The surgeon had so much confidence in the positive outcome of Riley's surgery that she had packed last night. As Bryn passed by their bed, she couldn't resist picking up Alex's stuffed bear, Harry. Harry had taken up permanent residence on their bed since the night she found Alex in the basement, clutching the bear tight. Bryn had insisted on bringing him upstairs against her lover's wishes. The blonde knew Lex was only trying to act tough. So from that night on, Harry, and Bryn's stuffed dog Noah, sat beside each other. Harry and Noah were a tangible reminder that Alex's and Bryn's hearts and souls had been linked together since childhood.

Bryn hugged the bear to her breast as she looked at another memento of their childhood. On the nightstand sat a photograph that Bryn had salvaged from Alex's memory box. Two smiling little girls were sitting on a hospital bed. Lex was delighted when Bryn had the print enlarged and framed, and placed prominently in their bedroom.

Bryn closed her eyes; remembering the day the picture was taken. Although outwardly, both children looked happy, Bryn knew that she had been terribly frightened.

"Lexi, I'm so scared." The little girl's lower lip trembled. Her precocious nature left her susceptible to fears that most four-year-olds never experienced. "What if your daddy can't fix my heart? I'll die if he can't. And what if I never wake up again? I won't see you anymore, and my mommy and daddy will be very sad." Tears spilled down the small face.

A small, slender hand reached for an even smaller hand in a gesture of friendship and comfort. "Now listen to me Bryn," Lexi replied wisely. "My dad will NOT let you die. Believe me, he's really good at his job—that's why your parents brought you all the way to Boston. They knew he could help you. Besides, you're my best friend...he'll take extra special care of you. So don't be scared...okay?" Alex kissed the little girl's cheek, and then carefully wiped the tears away.

Bryn sniffled. "Okay...if you say so, then I believe you. I love you, Lexi." She threw her arms around her friend, squeezing tight.

"I love you, too, Bryn. I'll love you forever."

Bryn set Harry back on the bed and sighed. She longed to help Alex get well emotionally. Lex had been an ardent supporter during the most painful and frightening time of her life, and she wanted to reciprocate. Bryn coveted an all encompassing lover's relationship with Alex. She wanted to be able to make love to Alex, in every sense of the word. But even if it never happened, she was determined to make their sexual encounters more 'interesting' for her lover. She blushed as images of what she had planned passed though her mind.

"Hi, Squeak." Her tall, gorgeous soul mate walked into the room. "Why is your face so red?" she asked as she gathered Bryn up in a huge bear hug.

"Um...no...no reason," she replied, returning the hug. "I'm so glad you're home," she enthused, changing the subject. "Thanks for calling me earlier about Riley. Is he still making a good recovery?"

Alex beamed. "He's doing great. Unless something unexpected comes up, we'll be able to leave in the morning." As she chatted with Bryn, the tall surgeon kicked off her shoes and changed into her favorite maroon, pullover sweater and jeans. Bryn was also wearing jeans, with an over-sized, gray Old Navy sweatshirt. "There. That feels much better. Let's grab a drink and head out to the porch—I'll fill you in on Riley's condition."

After obtaining a couple of bottles of Peach Snapple from the kitchen refrigerator, the two friends sat together on their enclosed patio. Alex settled her long legs across the coffee table, wiggling her bare toes contentedly.

"Feet hurt, honey?" Bryn asked sympathetically.

"Not too much. They're just really tired from standing all day." The surgeon sighed deeply. "Riley's surgery was incredibly tough. Working with those tiny coronary arteries was a real bear. But I expect him to make a full recovery." Alex chuckled softly. "Pretty soon he'll start growing like a weed."

"I'm so happy for him...and his parents. And for you, too. Lex. I've never seen you so affected by a case. I know you're always deeply caring of all your patients, but this child is different. What makes him so unique?"

Alex shrugged. "I don't really know. His parents were just so appreciative, and I felt good about doing what I could for them. I've always enjoyed helping people, saving lives, but this time was more special than usual. And I have to admit; I do feel proud about having the skills necessary to save him." Alex paused to wrap an arm around Bryn's shoulder. "Maybe the real reason is because I'm much happier in my personal life...thanks to a certain, very beautiful blonde I know." She tapped Bryn's nose. "What am I saying? I had no personal life...until I found you."

Bryn flushed with pleasure. "Lex...you can be such a sweetheart, sometimes. You know you have some of the staff at the hospital so fooled." She smiled, cupping Alex's cheek. "You still intimidate at least ninety percent of them. Little do they know what a pussy cat you are." She climbed onto Lex's lap, wrapping her arms around her lover's neck.

"Let them go on thinking I'm a bitch. I like it that way. I'll save my soft side for you and my patients." Alex leaned in for a tender kiss, which quickly turned passionate. When it ended, Alex spoke breathlessly. "Okay, you climbed on my lap, Bryn. You know what that means, don't you?"

"What?" Bryn feigned innocence.

"This." Alex gathered up Bryn and headed for their bedroom. The rest of the evening was spent in celebration of their love.

****

Bryn lay contentedly in Alex's arms as her tender lover slowly stroked her long, golden hair. The blonde inhaled deeply—the warm, sweet scent of her soul mate was like pure heaven. "Have I mentioned that I'm deeply and hopelessly in love with you, Alexandra Morgan?"

The surgeon chuckled. "Not since a few minutes ago. No, wait. That wasn't what you were yelling."

Bryn rolled to her side, bringing Alex with her. When she had gained access to her friend's shapely behind, she gave it a sharp smack.

"Ow. That really hurt. What was that for?"

"For teasing me. And quit looking so pitiful. I know you're faking."

Alex continued to pout. "You hit hard, Squeak.

On my naked butt, too. Check it to see if it's red."

Bryn began to caress Alex's behind. "There. I'm sorry, honey. It *is* a bit pink. Did it really hurt?"

"Gotcha," Alex teased. "I just really like it when you rub me there."

"You little rat. I can't resist your pouting, or your behind, and you know it. That's not playing fair."

"Rule 647. Whatever works is fair," the surgeon chuckled. "Listen...I'm starved. I'm going to get dressed and go out for some Chinese food. Does that sound good to you?"

"Mmm...Sounds great. We're all packed and ready for tomorrow. Maybe after dinner and some cocoa on the porch we should get some sleep."

"Good idea. I'm beat." Alex gave Bryn a quick kiss and got up to get dressed. "I won't be long."

****

A few hours later, the two women sat together on the porch, drinking their cocoa. It had become an important nightly ritual for them. They would discuss their day, their plans for the week, and their patients. Tonight the topic of conversation revolved around the upcoming trip to the Cape and plans to have a post Thanksgiving dinner with Bryn's family. The meal would be the weekend after Thanksgiving, but the O'Neill's didn't mind at all. They were looking forward to meeting the adult Alex—the woman who had captured their twenty eight-year-old daughter's heart.

"My parents are so excited about meeting you, Lex. I told them you looked quite a bit different than you did in 1975," Bryn giggled. "You've filled out considerably since then."

"Stop it, Bryn. Surely, you didn't tell them that." Alex looked worried.

"Yes, I did...but it's okay. They're used to me saying stuff like that."

"Bryn, you know I'm already nervous about seeing them for the first time in 24 years. And here you go embarrassing me before we're even introduced. It's important to me to make a good impression on your parents. What if they don't like me?" The dark brows furrowed and the insecurity was evident in Alex's expression.

"They'll love you. You make their 'baby girl' incredibly happy. You also helped me through a very difficult part of my childhood. Plus your father saved my life. They have to listen to me go on and on about how great you are over the phone each and every day. So I think it's pretty safe to say that they'll be ecstatic in my choice of a partner. And if the unthinkable happens, then that's just too bad. No one, not even Mom and Dad, can keep me away from you." Bryn snuggled closer to Alex.

"All right, then," Alex chuckled. "As usual, you've managed to make me feel better."

"As your soul mate, that's in my job description, Lex. I love you."

"I love you back, Squeak." Alex paused, touching her forehead to Bryn's. "You know, I'd like nothing better than to sit here with you all night, but I can't...I'm really tired. But before we go to bed, I'd like to call the hospital to check on Riley."

"Good idea. Otherwise, you won't sleep well."

Alex reached for the phone on the end table, and

then dialed quickly. "Dr. Morgan here. How's Riley Smith doing?" Alex stood up to pace around. She could never stay still when she was on the phone. "Yes...good...I want to be notified of the slightest problem immediately...you have my cell phone number...remember, it doesn't matter what time of the day or night it is...great...Happy Thanksgiving." The surgeon placed the phone back in its cradle.

Bryn looked expectantly at her lover with big green eyes. "How is he?"

Alex beamed. "Great...he's making an unusually fast recovery. Even so, I hate leaving him."

"Don't worry, honey. Stephanie will take good care of him." Bryn rubbed the surgeon's broad shoulders. "Let's go to bed. You can barely keep your eyes open."

"Okay, cute stuff."

Smiling at the term of endearment, Bryn took her lover's hand as they walked to their bedroom. Tomorrow was going to be a very special day for them. Their first holiday together—in their Cape Cod cottage. She couldn't wait.

****

The incessant ringing of the telephone woke Alex from a deep, contented sleep. She glanced at the bedside clock—it was just after midnight. "Dr. Morgan here." Her expression immediately turned grim. "What...No...that's not possible...he was doing just fine a couple of hours ago. I...I'm on my way. There has to be some kind of mistake." Trembling, Alex slammed down the phone and jumped out of bed.

"Lex?" Bryn asked sleepily. "What's wrong?" She rubbed her eyes, and tried to focus.

"The hospital called. Riley...Riley suddenly crashed. Bryn...they couldn't revive him." Alex's face twitched as she struggled to maintain control.

Tears streamed down Bryn's beautiful, sweet face. As Alex bent down to comfort her lover, the face suddenly turned into the angry, sneering countenance of Olivia Morgan.

Horrified, Alex gasped. "You bitch. What the hell are you doing here? And what have you done with Bryn?"

"Nothing. But it doesn't matter anyway. Bryn can't help you. No one can rescue you from the punishment you deserve. You're a murderer, Alexandra. You murdered my grandchild.

"You thought saving Riley could help you atone for the killing of your own baby, didn't you? Was it because Riley looked enough like you to be your own child? Well, forget it—nothing you do will ever make any difference. There's just no way you can receive forgiveness for your sins." Olivia laughed bitterly.

"Really, Alexandra. There's no sense in trying. Simply because you're slipping, you're not the surgeon you once were. You'll NEVER be the surgeon your father was. You couldn't save Riley—or Will. Remember Will—that little boy who died after YOU operated on him? Surely you didn't forget. You and your little bed warmer went to his funeral. You told his parents that you were so sorry. They said they didn't blame you, but they were lying. They knew why he died, and so do you. It was YOUR fault. You're being punished for that abortion. Will and Riley's *deaths are a part of that punishment.*

"But that's not all—there's more, isn't there? I know everything, all your dirty little secrets. You can't have normal sex, can you? You can't accept pleasure from anyone—not even your precious little Bryn. You're pitiful—you don't even realize how sick you are. It's pretty pathetic that the only way you can have an orgasm is to do it yourself. It's just as well, because you really should be alone. And you will— one day very soon. Because you'll never be able to allow Bryn to touch you. Just how long do you think Bryn will put up with your deviant behavior? Eventually, she'll leave you. You are an evil person, Alexandra. You deserve nothing but pain."

Alex huddled up in a little ball and began to scream. "Noooo. Nooo. I'm sorry...I'm so sorry. I didn't mean it...I didn't want to take my baby's life. I'm sorry. I'm...so...sorry."

"Oh, God, Lex. Please wake up. You're scaring me." Bryn was frantically trying to awaken her lover, who was moaning and thrashing from side to side. "It's okay, sweetheart...you're just dreaming."

Alex awakened with a start. She was terrified, and drenched with perspiration. "Riley...Riley died, Bryn. I couldn't save him." She looked around, desperately trying to get her bearings. "I...I failed him."

"Shh, he's just fine, honey." Bryn held Alex close, stroking her hair. "Remember? We called the hospital right before we went to bed." She felt her lover tremble. "Are you gonna be all right?"

"I don't know, Bryn. I...I need to call the hospital...just to make sure."

Poor baby. "I'll do it. You're too upset. I'm going to contact the hospital, then make us both some cocoa. Would you like to go out on the porch?"

Alex pursed her lips. She nodded, then got up to go into the bathroom to wash her face. Bryn went out to the kitchen to make the phone call while she prepared the cocoa. Ten minutes later, the two women sat huddled together on the couch.

Bryn put her arm around Alex's broad shoulders. "Riley is doing just fine, honey. He's improving steadily."

"Are you sure?"

"I'm sure. Lex, it was just a terrible nightmare." She patted her lover's shoulder. "Do you have any idea what triggered it? You haven't had one in a while."

Alex took a sip of cocoa. "It...it's my guilt over the abortion. Bonnie has been encouraging me to face up to it—that's all we talked about today. I didn't bring it up earlier because I didn't want to upset you. At first, she thought that fear was the only thing holding me back sexually. But now, she thinks there's more to it. And there is." Alex hung her head. "I...I don't..."

Bryn just listened carefully, rubbing Alex's back affectionately. "It's okay, honey. Go ahead."

"I don't deserve to feel pleasure, Bryn. Especially not from the one person I care about more than anyone else on this earth. A good, pure person who would have never taken her own child's life."

"Now, Lex. You listen to me..."

"No, hear me out. You asked me why Riley was so special. I didn't realize the real reason then, but I do now. In my subconscious mind, I associated Riley's life with my baby's. You must have noticed that Riley looks enough like me to be my own child. There's just one major difference—he's precious to his parents. They *want* him. No doubt they would give their life to save his. I didn't want my child, so I killed it. 'It'...how sad, I can't even tell you if my baby was a boy or a girl. I suppose I thought that if I saved Riley's life, I'd be one step closer to making up for killing my own child. But I'm still being eaten up with guilt. That's what the dream was about...I thought Riley had died. And Olivia was taunting me—about Riley, the abortion, and even Will. She...she told me nothing I do will ever make up for it. And she's right. I made a terrible mistake, and I deserve to be punished for it." Alex's face blanched, and her jaw twitched. Bryn knew that these were subtle signs that her lover was about to fall apart.

"No. You do NOT deserve to be punished. People do the best they can with the circumstances they're given." Bryn took Alex's hands in hers, trying to convey love and support. "Okay...you made a mistake. We all do...I know I have. We've been through all this before. If Olivia had loved and supported you, had been the kind of mother you needed, I don't believe you would have ever gone through with the abortion in the first place. Olivia gave you nothing—at a time when you needed everything from her. The only thing she ever gave you was an unbearable burden and a self-image totally at odds with who you really are. She never took the time to get to know the real Alexandra Morgan. The sad truth is, I seem to be the only one in this little Lex/Bryn/Olivia triangle who does know her. You certainly don't. The Alex Morgan I know places great value on human life. She is a wonderful, caring individual. For example, I found out through the hospital grapevine that the Smiths aren't the only family she's helped by donating her surgical skills."

Alex raised an eyebrow, surprised. She had always tried to keep that information confidential.

"If you're wondering how the staff found out, it's because the families told them. They wanted to share with everyone what a generous thing you did. It's only natural for people to talk about unusual acts of kindness. And you're the woman they were talking about. You're incredibly kind and generous. When I look at you...I see the most remarkable, warm, and loving person I've ever known. A person that deserves to be happy. Please...let her be happy, Lex." Bryn's voice dropped to a whisper. "Will you forgive her? She's already suffered enough."

The distraught woman considered Bryn's question thoughtfully. After long moments, Alex responded, barely above a whisper. "Yes. I think I can now. Bryn?"

"What, honey?"

"I..." She choked back a sob. "Will you hold me...please?"

"Always, Lex." Bryn opened her arms and gathered her lover to her breast. Unable to hold back the tears any longer, Alex broke down. The agony in her soul was profound, and she cried for a long time. Bryn held her close as her own heart broke at the pain Alex had endured. Her soothing voice and gentle touch settled over Alex like a warm blanket, and something wonderful happened. The frightened little girl inside the stoic surgeon grew *strong*. After the storm, the sun began to rise.

Chapter 21

Bryn sat back in her seat, relaxing. *First class is definitely the way to fly.* Her eyes were closed as she listened to the music through her headphones. Alex's hand rested on Bryn's arm while she scanned a medical journal. The surgeon seemed to be coping well after last night's horrific nightmare. Being able to lean on Bryn for emotional help made her burden much easier to handle.

Putting aside the journal, Alex squirmed as she tried to get comfortable. She tapped Bryn on the shoulder, but the petite blonde was completely lost in her music.

"Huh? What is it, Lex?"

"Do you have any Ibuprofen? My legs are aching from standing so long during Riley's surgery. Not to mention the fact that there's never enough room for me on an airplane."

"Sure, sweetheart. Look in my bag—I'm sure I

packed some."

Alex reached under Bryn's seat, and pulled up a large, black leather travel bag—with several deep pockets. "Oh hell," Alex muttered, as she placed the satchel in her lap. "This will be like trying to find a needle in a haystack. I can't see a damned thing." She decided to let her fingers do the walking. Suddenly, she jumped. Alex was startled to detect something quite a bit larger than a needle, and it was moving. *What the hell is vibrating in here? I know she didn't pack my pager. What on earth?*

Alex's blue eyes grew wide with shock as her hand settled around a distinctive, cylindrical shaped object. *Ooo. Bryn, what do you have in mind for our first Thanksgiving together? If it's what I think it is, I'm going to have a lot to be thankful for.*

Turning the vibrator off, her lover smirked at Bryn. After closing the bag, she again tapped the unsuspecting blonde on the shoulder. One eyebrow disappeared into the dark bangs. "Um...Squeak. I can't find the Ibuprofen. But there was something else in there. Perhaps you intended it for medicinal purposes. However, it's not quite what I was looking for." Her silky voice lowered an octave. "At least not right now."

"What are you talking...?" Bryn quickly turned pale, and then blushed a deep red all the way to her blond roots. "Oh, shh...shoot. I didn't mean to throw that in there. I thought I put it in my suitcase. Where is it? Did you put it back?" she asked frantically.

Alex burst into laughter. "Don't worry. It's safely tucked away." She leaned over and whispered in her lover's ear, "Where did *that* thing come from?

You naughty girl."

Bryn giggled shyly. "From a website I found. I was planning on surprising you...with, um...a few things."

Alex's big, blue eyes grew wide with wonder. "A few things? You mean there's more?"

"Maybe," Bryn teased.

"Oh. Well, I was definitely surprised. And I have to admit that I'm very intrigued. My innocent little Squeak. You never stop surprising me. I'm so glad we're together." Alex leaned over for a quick, discreet kiss. "You make every single day of my life so much fun. I think I'll keep you."

"So...you really don't mind? You...like the idea?" Bryn asked nervously.

"Oh yes, very much. And I like you, too."

"Right back at ya, Lex." She tapped Alex's nose, then cleared her throat. "Let me find that Ibuprofen for you now. I can't have my favorite doctor hurting. I need you in good shape for our walks on the beach—and *other* things."

Alex smiled. "Your little surprise made me forget all about my aching legs. Now, let's see. What else have you got in there?" The surgeon reached for the bag in delight.

Bryn swatted Alex's hand. "Lex. Behave yourself. Later."

****

Alex maneuvered the rented jeep into the driveway of her childhood home. She swallowed audibly at the bittersweet homecoming, willing her wildly beating heart to slow down. She wasn't going to allow her painful memories to spoil the holiday for Bryn. Taking a deep breath, she finally spoke. "Well, Squeak...what do you think?"

Bryn couldn't contain her delight. "It's gorgeous, Lex." She threw her arms around her lover, hugging her tight.

The gray and white clapboard Cape Cod residence was situated on Old Silver beach in Falmouth, a quaint little village. The house on the ocean had been immaculately maintained. In addition to a fresh coat of paint, a spacious, screened in porch had recently been added.

The two women got out of the car, and sauntered hand in hand up the steps. Alex unlocked the front door and pushed it open before suddenly pulling Bryn into her arms for a long, slow, tender kiss. The blonde's knees grew weak. When their lips finally parted, Alex looked into smoky green eyes. "I've never cared about anyone the way I care about you— you've changed my whole world. I've never felt so complete." Alex scooped Bryn up and walked into the living room. She sat down on the couch, her precious bundle still in her arms. "I'm never letting go of you. You know that, right?"

"Right. And make sure that you keep that promise. I don't want to be out of your arms all weekend." Bryn slipped her tongue into Alex's warm, soft mouth. She ached to make love to this woman in every way imaginable: to touch her, to feel her, to taste her.

Hmm. Something's different about the way Lex is responding to me, something different in her whole demeanor. Whatever it is, I definitely like it. Maybe my wish will come true...and soon.

The dark haired woman reluctantly pulled away, breathless. "Hey...there are a few things we need to do. I want you to see the rest of the house. We can kiss all weekend, once we're settled. Let's get the luggage." Alex grinned crookedly at her lover, tapping the blonde's nose.

"Okay...first we retrieve our suitcases, second you give me the grand tour—a quick one, and then we can get down to business." Bryn smirked playfully.

After putting their luggage away, Alex guided Bryn through each room of their completely re-decorated and re-furbished cottage. Their final stop was the kitchen. While Alex made the coffee, Bryn discovered a box of Pinwheels sitting on the kitchen counter. "You've thought of everything, Lex." She opened the package of cookies and prepared a tray for them. When the coffee finished brewing, Alex carried the tray out to the porch.

"I can't believe how beautiful it is here. The ocean view is spectacular." Bryn munched her cookie happily. "It's so romantic, too."

"I knew you would love it. I've imagined bringing you here...from the first moment we met in Atlanta...before I even remembered you were my Squeak."

Bryn smirked. "You were interested in me, Lex? Right from the beginning?"

Alex blushed. "Oh, yes...I admit it. It was love at first sight for me." She chuckled. "The night you brought your thesis to my house—when I was so sick, and you took such good care of me...I didn't want you to leave...ever."

"Well, that makes two of us. I had a huge crush on you from the first day you walked into I.C.U. I couldn't believe that the 'Ice Princess' I had heard so much about, and the Alex Morgan I knew was the same person. Underneath that frosty exterior, you have the warmest heart I've ever known." Bryn moved closer, using her fingers to wipe away a bit of chocolate from her soul mate's full lips.

Alex captured Bryn's fingers in her mouth, sucking sensuously. "Mmm," Bryn moaned. "And your mouth is just as warm." *She's trying to drive me crazy today. Or seduce me...or both.*

Alex removed each finger from her mouth slowly, then kissed Bryn's palm. "Later on, I'll show you just how warm it can be," she replied in a deep, silky tone.

The petite blonde fanned herself. "I...I'll look forward to it," she stammered. The air fairly crackled with tension.

Alex grinned; elated with the effect she was having on her partner and on herself. "Ready for a long walk on the beach? It'll help us work up an appetite for the lobster and champagne dinner I've ordered. My favorite local restaurant is catering it."

"Ooo. I love lobster and champagne. That's a wonderful surprise." Bryn climbed into Alex's lap, hugging her.

"I thought you'd like it. Now hop off before we both end up somewhere else."

"That's the whole idea. Okay...beach first, bed later." The two stood up, laughing. "I'll race you, Lex."

"You're on." The two women sprinted down to

the ocean. Alex's long legs gave her an unfair advantage, and she made it first.

"Lexi. Can't you let me win...just once, Miss-Legs-Are-Longer-Than-Mine?"

One eyebrow went up. Alex's smirk quickly turned into a pout. "Can I help it if you're vertically challenged? Anyway, I kind of like things this way. Makes it easier to carry you." The surgeon lifted Bryn into her arms again, and spun her around and around. The laugh was on her when she got dizzy, and they both fell onto the sand, laughing. Alex looked into Bryn's beautiful green eyes and smiled. "If this were a private beach, I'd have my way with you right now, you know."

"Ooo...is that a threat or a promise?"

"It's a promise."

"Well, too bad it's not private, then. But I dare you to kiss me."

Seldom one to pass up a challenge, and certainly not one presented in such a beautiful package, Alex leaned toward Bryn. As their lips met, she was almost overcome by a fire in the center of her being. She felt a passion like never before. Alex realized that if she didn't experience the physical pleasure that only her lover could give, her spirit would soon wither and die. For so long, her soul had been parched and barren. Bryn's touch was the only thing that could nourish and restore it. Her soul mate's physical love was the last step necessary to complete her healing. And she was finally ready.

The kiss was so deep and intense, that Bryn couldn't help but sense that something was about to change in their relationship. Lex seemed to have released all her doubts, fears, and insecurities as she connected with Bryn on a spiritual level as well. The two women felt closer than they had ever been. At last, their lips parted. Blue eyes gazed into green with love.

"I...I guess we'd better continue with our walk, sweetheart. Those people over there are staring." Alex grazed her thumb across Bryn's full lips.

"Did...did you just call me sweetheart?"

The surgeon blushed. "Yes, I guess I did."

"That's just fine by me, Lex. Let's come to the beach more often. I like what it does to you." Alex helped Bryn stand up, and they brushed the sand from their clothes. Hand in hand, they continued their walk down the beach—dark hair and light hair contrasting sharply in the November sun.

Chapter 22

The two women sat in their dining room, enjoying their first Thanksgiving dinner together. The beautifully set table glowed with candlelight and happy faces. Alex poured more champagne for Bryn.

"This dinner is wonderful, Lex. Everything has been perfect ever since we arrived. I'm having so much fun."

Alex grinned crookedly. "Same here. I don't know when I've been so relaxed. We'll have to come here every chance we get." She sipped her champagne thoughtfully, her expression turning serious. "There's something I have to confess to you, Squeak."

The blonde nodded, patting her friend's arm. "Go ahead."

"I was frightened to be here again. When we first arrived, my heart was beating so rapidly I could hardly breathe. Then...I just thought of you, and why we were here, and how much we care about each other...and..." She lifted Bryn's hand, kissing it tenderly. "Having you here took all the sting away, and I realized how happy I am...because of you. This is our home now, and we're going to make many wonderful memories here. I can't even come close to telling you how good I feel right now."

Bryn's green eyes sparkled. In the last few months, she had watched Alex slowly transform into an emotionally whole person. In some ways, she was like a completely different woman. Bryn decided to take a chance, to go with her gut feelings. She climbed onto her lover's lap, whispering in her ear. "I can make you feel even better," she purred. The blonde traced Alex's ear with her tongue. "Would you like that?"

Alex shuddered, her body set aflame by her lover's words. "Oh, God. Yes. Please, Bryn. I want it...now."

"Okay," she whispered. Bryn nibbled her neck, slowly making her way toward Alex's breasts. "Upstairs?"

"Mmm....I don't think....I can walk...up the stairs." Alex breathed heavily, helpless under Bryn's touch. "Family room...fireplace."

Bryn managed to tear herself away from her lover's delicious neck and led Alex into the next room. She pulled two large down throws from the couch, and spread them out in front of the fire. Alex, flushed with anticipation, leaned down toward her lover. Bryn took the face she adored into trembling hands—peppering it with tender kisses. "You can't imagine how much I've longed to cradle you in my arms and make love to you."

Alex could only moan as Bryn kept up her tender ministrations. "Thank you...ohhh...for being so...patient...with me."

"Anything for you...my Lex, anything." She claimed her soul mate's lips again, kissing them deeply. As the kiss grew more passionate, she unbuttoned Alex's shirt and loosened the ties of her drawstring pants. Two small hands slipped into the waistband of Alex's underwear, and Bryn caressed her lover's shapely behind.

Eyes closed in ecstasy, Alex mumbled, "Oh...that feels...oh, Bryn." Her knees turned to rubber, and she slipped down to the soft pallet by the fire. Her soul mate eased Alex to the floor and straddled the beautiful woman. Bryn was assertive and confident. She had fantasized about this moment and knew exactly how she wanted to proceed. But...it had to be right for her lover.

"I want so much to please you, darling. Everything has to be perfect for you. Tell me...how do you want it?" she whispered, as she began stroking Alex's breasts.

"I...I want..." she panted.

"Go ahead. Tell me." Her lover whispered in the blonde's ear. Bryn's eyes grew wide, and she swallowed hard. "Oh, God."

"Bryn?" Alex moaned.

"What?"

"Please...hurry. I've waited long enough already." The surgeon was beside herself with need, rocking her hips involuntarily against her lover.

"Whatever you want, my love. I'll take care of you right away." Trembling, Bryn shed her own clothes and finished undressing her partner. Staring at the gorgeous body beneath her, she caught her breath. "You are so beautiful, Lex."

"Please touch me...touch me now." The blue eyes were so needy and vulnerable, that Bryn thought she would melt. Nodding, she positioned herself above Alex, capturing a nipple in her mouth. She suckled gently, as her hand slowly moved down the flat belly. When she arrived at her destination, skilled fingers stroked the folds of skin that lay beneath her lover's soft, dark curls.

Alex gasped, then moaned at the intense sensation. No one had touched her there in so long—and never anyone she was deeply in love with. The feeling was beyond incredible. "Oh, God. I can't believe you're touching me. It's even better than I imagined."

"You like?"

"Mmm...yes."

Bryn was thrumming with passion herself—finally being able to caress her lover intimately was an exquisite sexual experience. She felt so soft and warm—and so wet. She continued to stroke, wanting to take things slow.

Alex had other ideas. "Please, Bryn. I need you inside me...right now. I'm sorry, but I just can't wait."

"Okay," she whispered, her voice cracking. Bryn gently entered her. As her hips rose up to meet her lover's finger, Alex cried out. "Is this what you need?," the blonde teased.

"Yes...oh, yes. But I need more. Please." She rocked her hips impatiently.

Bryn had never seen Alex this aroused before. She slipped in two, then three fingers. Her lover cried out again at the sensation of being deliciously filled. Alex's beautiful face was bathed in passion, the tendons in her neck standing out. She looked as if she was in pain, but nothing could have been further from the truth. She was in complete rapture. For the first time in her life, experiencing the ecstasy that comes with the expression of true love. As Alex got closer to orgasm, Bryn increased her ministrations, holding her partner very close. She wanted her to feel as secure as possible.

"Oh, God, Bryn. That feels...ohhh...so...so good. Please, don't stop." The beautiful woman quivered with anticipation. She was moaning continuously now, the delicious pressure inside her building rapidly.

Bryn was on fire. Alex was incredibly responsive, and the cries and moans she was drawing from the dark haired beauty were threatening to send her over the edge as well. All she cared about was her partner's pleasure. The blonde leaned down, and suckled her lover's dark nipple again while increasing the speed of her hand. The warm suction, coupled with the deep motions of skilled fingers, finally sent Alex crashing over the edge. The sensations were so intense, that the normally stoic woman completely lost all control. She arched her back and screamed Bryn's name—over and over again. When the tremors finally subsided, Alex collapsed, panting, in her lover's arms. She burrowed her face in Bryn's neck, totally overwhelmed.

We made it, Lex. Together. The blonde immediately felt hot tears on her neck. "Hey, are you okay, honey?" She kissed the top of the dark head. "I promise not to let go of you."

"I...I can't talk...right now."

"Then don't. Just let me hold you close for a while." Bryn was trembling inside. No one had ever responded to her lovemaking as Lex had. They lay together for a long time beside the waning fire, enjoying the warmth of each other's body.

Alex finally pulled away, wiping her eyes. She looked at Bryn and smiled at her, tenderly stroking her cheek. "Wow...that was...exquisite. Thank you...you've mended my heart. I feel..." She stifled a sob. "I feel...complete." She pulled Bryn to her breast, hugging her tight. "I love you, my Squeak."

"I love you, too, Lex." Bryn started crying.

"Hey. What's wrong, sweetheart?" Alex rocked her tenderly, kissing the soft blonde hair. "You know how much I hate it when you cry."

"I'm...I'm just so relieved...and I...I was afraid I couldn't please you...and I was...so scared for you," She hiccupped.

"Scared? Why?" Alex crooned.

"In case I failed you. I didn't want to see you hurt anymore...I...I couldn't bear it." Bryn wept, too emotional to speak.

Alex's heart melted. "Now listen. Your lovemaking exceeded my wildest dreams. It was wonderful...and I wasn't afraid anymore. I begged you to touch me, and when you did, it was more than I ever expected." She chuckled. "Hopefully, I didn't break any windows around here." Alex ducked her head, blushing. "The important thing is that you gave me much more than incredible sex. You gave me the courage to face my fears, and to conquer them." She caressed her lover's soft cheek. "You told me before that we could work things out, and you were right...as usual." Alex grinned crookedly. "Now dry those tears, and let's go find our dessert. It's white chocolate mousse with raspberries," she teased.

Bryn stopped crying and smiled. "You always did know how to cheer me up. Ice cream when we were little, and white chocolate mousse now."

"Hey, I have to know what my best girl likes. Now let's go eat that dessert. We have a lot of exploring to do before morning." Alex winked devilishly. "By the way, where'd you put that black satchel?"

Bryn giggled. "I'll go get it as soon as we finish eating our mousse. But maybe you should consider reinforcing our windows first, Lex."

"Let 'em break."

"By the time I get through with you, they'll all be broken," Bryn purred.

Alex swallowed hard. "Um...Bryn? Maybe we should forget the dessert for now."

****

Sunrise found them in each other's arms; dreaming of the love they had shared. Two mended hearts— joined together forever.

The petite blonde sighed contentedly as she curled up on the couch with her cup of cocoa. Blissfully happy, she watched the waves break onto the shore, the pleasant sound almost lulling her to sleep. Last night had been like a dream come true. She and

Lex had spent the entire night exploring a brand new level of intimacy. Bryn felt like writing poetry about it. Their lovemaking had always been wonderful—but now...it was...magic.

"I wish you'd hurry home, my love," she spoke aloud. "I miss you." Alex had driven to Children's Hospital in Boston to call on a former colleague. Bryn remained behind, exhausted from the previous night's adventure.

Lex, on the other hand, seemed rejuvenated. As Bryn had kissed her goodbye, she was fairly glowing—happy, confident, and totally at peace with herself. Just like the Lexi of long ago.

Bryn's pleasant memories were interrupted by the sound of the front door closing. "Lex? Is that you, honey?"

"Honey?" A tall, striking woman with shoulder-length, chestnut colored hair, and large hazel eyes, stepped onto the screened in porch. She was immaculately dressed, and very attractive. Bryn immediately recognized her from the cold stare on her face.

"Olivia Morgan? What are you doing here? In our home?" The blonde eyed her cautiously.

"I'm here to see Alexandra—my daughter. And who on earth are you?"

The sweet blonde exploded in anger. "Well, you're out of luck. *Lex* isn't here right now. Allow me to introduce myself—again. I'm Bryn O'Neill. I don't suppose you remember me. I was a heart patient of your husband's at Children's Hospital in 1975—and your daughter's best friend. But, thanks to you, she lost me. Fortunately, just a few months ago, we found one another again. And now we're more than just childhood chums. A whole lot more. In fact, we're *lovers*. And this house you just waltzed into, belongs to us. So hand over that key and leave. Otherwise, I'll have to call the police and have them arrest you for breaking and entering. Oh, just one more thing: be sure and let the door hit your prim little ass on the way out."

Olivia gasped, fanning herself. "Why you little..." She sank down onto a chair, in shock. "You...and Alexandra...you're..."

"Gay is the word I believe you were looking for. Yep, we definitely are. You're shocked, no doubt. How could you have known? You never paid the right kind of attention to your daughter to find out. Of course, there's a lot about her you never even bothered to find out about. For instance, did you know she's one of the most respected and skilled pediatric heart surgeons in the country? And that she sometimes performs her services for free? No? Didn't think so. Did you also know that she's very tough and stoic on the outside, but very tenderhearted on the inside? That she loves Chinese food, Pinwheels, anything blueberry, horses, dogs, children, old movies, The Red Sox, snow, and most of all, me? That she suffers from migraine headaches when she's upset. That she has a sensitive stomach? That she worshipped and emulated her father?"

"I...I..." Olivia was completely speechless. For some reason, the tiny blonde spitfire intimidated and unnerved her.

"Did you also know that after a long week of surgery, her shoulder aches so much that it wakes her up at night?"

"What...what do you mean?" Olivia's face grew pallid.

"That's right...the one you dislocated. It's starting to give her some problems."

Olivia gasped.

"Yes. She remembered everything. It took a lot of love and therapy, but she finally remembered."

"It was just an accident," she replied coldly.

"Sure. You go on believing that if you want to, Olivia."

"You have no right. No right at all."

"Don't I? I have every right. You do realize that I've given Lex the love and acceptance that you never gave her. I've held her through many dark nights of pain and despair. Encouraged her to show her emotions. Dried her tears. Taught her how to *feel* again. And for the first time since her father died, she is a complete, whole, happy individual. She managed to survive a childhood almost totally barren of tenderness and affection, to become a compassionate and skilled heart surgeon. David Morgan would be so proud."

"Yes. I believe he would." A tall figure entered the room. Alex Morgan gave her mother a withering look. "I see we have an uninvited guest, Bryn—in our home."

"Yes, sweetheart. But I've taken care of it. Olivia was just leaving. After all, this is supposed to be a happy home." She moved over to Lex, putting an arm around her supportively. Instantly, she could sense that her strong partner was capable of handling things on her own.

Alex sighed. "Why are you here, Olivia? Bryn

and I have plans—and they don't include you."

"I imagine you do have plans, however perverted they are. You...you and your little...girlfriend. I always knew there was something sick about your relationship. And I was right."

"Now you just wait one God damned minute," Bryn fumed. "Our childhood friendship was just that—a beautiful friendship—innocent and pure. Of course, someone like you wouldn't understand that. You're a cold, heartless, bitch."

Alex smirked, thoroughly enjoying her feisty partner's defense of her. She had never heard Bryn swear before now.

"How rude can you be? You barely know me." Olivia was flabbergasted.

"Don't I? I know enough. Usually, I make it a rule not to judge a person before I actually meet them. But when it comes to Lex, I'm afraid all my rules just fly out the window. And speaking of rules, I'm this close to breaking my rule of non-violence." Bryn held up her thumb and index finger. "The only thing keeping me from slapping you senseless, is that I wouldn't touch you with a ten foot pole."

"Alexandra Devin. Are you just going to stand by and let her talk to me this way?"

"Um...let me think for a minute. Sure...why not?" she replied coolly.

"How can you treat me this way? Allowing this, this *woman* to be so disrespectful to your own mother. And what have you done to turn your brother against me? He won't even speak to me anymore."

Alex laughed bitterly. "David must have finally gotten a ball transplant. It's about damn time, too."

Bryn bit her lip to keep from laughing.

Olivia turned pale with rage. "You always did have a foul mouth, Alexandra."

Alex shrugged. "Sorry. You just bring out the best in me. And by the way, Olivia. It's Alex—not Alexandra." The tall surgeon pulled her lover close. "Now...if you'll excuse us, Bryn and I have a life to live together—a life that will never include you."

"Oh, dear God. I've got to get some fresh air." Olivia turned to leave. "You'll be hearing from me."

"You can let yourself out, Olivia," Bryn snickered.

Alex looked at Bryn in complete awe. No one had ever gotten the best of Olivia the way her sweet natured partner had just done.

When the door finally closed, Bryn hugged Alex tight. "I'm so proud of you. You were so cool. And you didn't even mention the accident. How can you be so calm after all she's done to you?"

"I surprised myself. Alex Morgan—the bitch on wheels. I've had to fight every battle, climb every hill alone...since my father died. Three months ago I would have simply pushed you aside and ripped Olivia's heart out." She gently took Bryn's face in her hands. "But my own personal angel showed me that I could share my burdens, and that it's not a sign of weakness to ask for help. Walking in on you confronting Olivia made me realize I didn't need to yell and scream and throw things at her. All I needed to do was tell Olivia I don't give a damn about her—and that her opinion means zip to me. And, I did that.

"It's over. You said I needed to forgive her. To be truthful, I haven't. I'm not sure if I ever can. But

I don't hate her anymore. She's in the past, Squeak. I'm ready to move forward with my life—my life with you. What do you think about us having our commitment ceremony on New Year's Eve? We'll start the Millennium together." She took Bryn's hand and opened the door. The soul mates walked toward the beach.

"Sounds like the best idea I've heard all day. You and Mom and I can start planning it as soon as we get back to Atlanta. Of course, we also have to get a Christmas tree for our house."

"And pick out two dogs," Alex added as they made their way to the ocean.

"And buy season tickets to see the National League Champion Braves," Bryn enthused.

Alex tried to stifle a smile. "I already did that. It was supposed to be a surprise, but I couldn't resist telling you. I'll hand over the tickets as soon as you promise to go with me to Fenway Park to see my Red Sox."

Bryn gave her beautiful lover a huge hug and a kiss. "I promise. You're such a sweetheart. Thank you, Lex. We have so much to look forward to together."

"Yes, Squeak. We do. Oh...I almost forgot. I phoned Stephanie while I was in Boston. She said that Riley had been moved to a regular room." Alex grinned crookedly. "He guzzled down an entire bottle of formula for his first Thanksgiving dinner."

Bryn beamed. "That's great. His mom and dad must be so happy—almost as happy as we are. I can't believe we've come this far in only a few months."

"In reality, it took twenty-four years. Don't forget that tomorrow we're going back for a visit to Children's Hospital—where it all began." Alex faced Bryn, taking her in her arms tenderly. "Best friends forever?"

"Best friends...forever and ever."

Coming next from
Yellow Rose Books

Tiopa Ki Lakota
By D. Jordan Redhawk

Immerse yourself into the culture of the Lakota Indians. Watch as the daughter of a warrior, fulfills a shaman's prophecy and is on her way to becoming a warrior and hunter. During a rite of passage, the warrior, Anpo, has a vision of a woman with hair the color of the sun who will play an important part in her future. It is several years later, when two groups come together for a hunt that the white woman, Kathleen, a captured slave, first appears. She soon becomes the woman of the warrior when a white buffalo is slain. Together they begin a journey that must ease language barriers, blend cultural differences and form a bond that forges their own path to love.

Available October 2000

Available soon from
Yellow Rose Books

Bar Girls
By Jules Kurre

Keagan Donovan is a taciturn English major. Keeping control of her emotions has always been second nature until the aspiring writer meets Rudy, a fellow English major, in a local bar. Keagan and Rudy find they have a lot in common but as they spend more time together, Keagan's insecurities contiune to keep them at arm's length. Will Rudy have the patience to deal with Keagan's inconsistent behavior? Will Keagan be able to overcome her fears and accept Rudy unconditionally into her life?

Tumbleweed Fever
By L. J. Maas

In the Oklahoma Territory of the old west Devlin Brown is trying to redeem herself for her past as an outlaw, now working as a rider on a cattle ranch. Sarah Tolliver is a widow with two children and a successful ranch, but no way to protect it from the ruthless men who would rather see her fail. When the two come together sparks fly, as a former outlaw loses her heart to a beautiful yet headstrong young woman.

Seasons: Book Two
By Anne Azel

Book Two, containing the stories Spring Rains and Summer Heat, continues the saga of Robbie and Janet Williams. Robbie has a career in the film industry while Janet is an educator. Seasons examines the crises that can come into the average woman's life, and focuses on the courage it takes to be female and/or gay in today's society.

Lost Paradise
By Francine Quesnel

Kristina Von Deering is a young, wealthy Austrian stuntwoman working on an Austrian/Canadian film project in Montreal. On location, she meets and eventually falls in love with a young gopher and aspiring camerawoman named Nicole McGrail. Their friendship and love is threatened by Nicole's father who sees their relationship as deviant and unnatural. He does everything in his power to put an end to it.

Other titles to look for in the
coming months from
Yellow Rose Books

None So Blind By L. J. Maas
(Winter 2000)

Encounter Series By Anne Azel
(Winter 2000)

Safe Harbor By Radclyffe
(Winter 2000)

Dr. Livingston, I Presume By T. Novan
(Winter 2001)

Daredevil Hearts By Francine Quesnel
(Winter 2001)

Prairie Fire By L. J. Maas
(Winter 2001)

Hope's Path By Carrie Carr
(Winter 2001)

Storm Front By Belle Reilly
(Summer 2001)

Alix Stokes resides in the Deep South. Her hobbies include reading, writing, listening to music, attending baseball games and the theater, and playing with her two dogs. She loves spending time with her family and adores animals of almost every kind. Her dream is to continue writing, and to one day become an amateur puppeteer.

Printed in the United States
2935